The Bookkeeper's Daughter

FAREH IQBAL

Prologue

I have stories.

They hide behind my eyes, peek from under my lashes, flutter across my fingertips and are forever imprinted in my heart.

When I try to capture them in ink, the words slip away and the paper remains an empty canvas waiting for the right shades of colour to paint a tale.

A tale about a girl.

And a boy.

And Time.

About a season of love, and a season of loss.

About a journey that changed my life forever.

A journey that changed me forever.

Chapter I
The Bookkeeper's Daughter

Ray was nervous. Restless. She couldn't stop cracking her fingers, tapping her feet, pulling at her messy ponytail. She could feel something terribly wrong was about to happen.

Women's intuition, perhaps? She didn't know, it felt like the time her parents planned a 'surprise trip' to 'somewhere fantastic' and twenty minutes later she wound up bound to a white plastic chair watching the steady approach of the dentist with a crocodile smile and an injection.

That night did not turn out well.

She shivered. And here she was again, years later, no cavities, but the same feeling. The feeling that there was something lurking, an unseen force beyond the realm of her control but not beyond her psyche. It felt overwhelming. She walked four steps across her bedroom floor and opened the window; a rush of crisp, winter air lifted her hair off her shoulders. She felt calmer looking out into the December sky, where Dawn was stretching her golden wings. Calmer, but still restless.

Maybe she just felt alone.

But she wasn't alone was she? There was a world full of books downstairs in her father's shop and a stray cat that sometimes came by mewling for a crumb and a saucer of milk. Ray had named the affectionate black cat, Molly. And truly these visits made Ray's days a little more meaningful and a little less lonely.

But try as she might, her one way conversations with Molly were about as enlightening as one would expect from an unresponsive feline. There was something missing. Something she could only define as a spark. And someone to ignite that flame.

There was no one in Ray's life that she could call her own. Not really. Not after her father had passed away. His absence had left a dull ache that never quite left her side. And then there was her mother. Oh, Eleanor. Aside from their overall bone structure and matching dark eyes tinged with grey irises, there were no similarities between herself and her mother. And that was a good thing, Ray assured herself as she stepped away from the window.

Though the sky was brightening with pale shades of blue the wind had taken on a bitter turn. This would have been the perfect day to curl up in front of a fireplace with a cup of bubbling hot chocolate with someone lovely. Ray closed her eyes. Maybe Molly was free later.

It wasn't as though she was waiting for a prince to rescue her. She was fine. Really and truly fine. It was just a strange sort of reality to come to terms with when you spent your whole life surrounded by the promises of happily ever after, ingrained in almost every book you ever read. She was so used to being alone that to fathom anything different was almost impossible.

The height of romance and courtship these days for Ray's generation was being someone's number one friend on Snapchat, or equally ridiculous, favoriting their Tweets or liking all of their Instagram pictures. What does that even mean? Ray shook her head. No. The social media aspect of relationships was not appealing to her at all. But because she wasn't a part of the scene, she felt even more isolated from everything. Sometimes standing your ground and not caving into expectations and apps made her feel even lonelier. It wasn't what she wanted but she had yet to figure out what it was she *did* want.

Ray turned away from the window and allowed the waning heat of the morning sun to warm her back. She felt solid, human. There was no fairy tale, no prince, all the visions vanished before her eyes and she could hear the sound of hooves fading away, though once she could have sworn they were coming to rescue her.

Because right now she was seeing castles in the sky and sinking on earthly plains.

Maybe this was the end. It felt like the end and she was forced to come to terms with the fact that there was no grand Comedic ending. That her life was utterly ordinary. The drawbridge was closing, there was no prince charming courageously battling a fire breathing dragon to rescue her from the monotony of her daily life. Even though her third year fairy tale seminar in university had taught her that most heroines were almost always at the mercy of a knight errant, and while everyone had managed to identify themselves with the princess, Ray had adamantly refused to see herself that way.

Not as Andersen's mermaid who gave up her father and fins for a man who could not love her in return; nor as Sleeping Beauty whose whole world was slipping between dreams as she awaited true love's kiss to rescue her from her slumber; her hair was the wrong shade for her to be cast as

8

Rapunzel, anxiously waiting for her prince to save her from the evil witch who locked her up in an ivory tower, a mere spectator of the world below. She didn't believe in fairy godmothers, so Cinderella was out of the question. She didn't really understand what was going on with Snow White. She ate a poisoned apple, slept, woke up and fell for the first guy that kissed her. What about compatibility? What about going steady? What about finding out someone's favorite color before proposing matrimony?

Some stories were ridiculous. But some stories, oh some stories held the promise of happiness and adventure and true love locked within a paperback seal. Alas, the only experience she had pertaining to the world of romance were in the pages of books.

Even though Ray didn't see herself as a victimized female protagonist in the pages of a Brothers Grimm fairy tale, magical lands, castles guarded by dangerous beasts, redemptive love, prince charming were all the ripe ingredients to shape her fantasies of what love meant. It was only until now that Ray realized that she no longer saw herself as the heroine, but it didn't mean that she didn't believe in the happily ever after it endorsed. Such power in words, such hope in language, perhaps there was more to it than she was giving it credit for.

The thing was, she honestly believed in it. But if that was the case then why hadn't it happened to her yet? She felt like she was endlessly waiting for something magical to happen and it only seemed to be real when she was curled up in bed reading. Not in her waking life.

Speaking of her waking life, she really ought to get dressed and tend to her bookshop downstairs. Ray looked around her tiny room, tucked away upstairs and wondered where she had last seen her shoes. The wooden floors were covered with a faded blue rug and her reliable desk, which took up as much space as her bed, stood in the corner overflowing with papers and a laptop that was hidden underneath the debris of books. She didn't even think her laptop was even charged. When was the last time she had even used it? With a deft motion she flicked up the screen and pressed the 'on' button. The screen went white and she saw her word document with random lines strewn over the page.

Her novel. What a joke.

Ray sighed and rubbed the back of her neck as she tried to make sense of the haphazard words that danced across the screen. 'Songs in the distance,' 'Dirt and dreams' 'Where do dreams go when we awaken?' She chewed her bottom lip and shut the screen with a firm click. Her novel would remain unfinished. There was nothing she could articulate well enough to say. Why did she think she could even write? Graduating with an English Degree, albeit from the University of Bath, didn't mean one had the talent, skill and magical voice to weave stories. It just meant you survived four years of school, wrote over seventy essays, read over two hundred books and came out alive. Along the way, yes of course, she had soaked up information like a sponge and fallen in love with the words of Goethe, Keats, Byron and loved every moment of her Jane Austen seminar course. But she had come out the same way she gone in, struggling to write her heart's desires.

Perhaps that was why she was filled with apprehension and anxiety this morning, because she was aware and had resigned herself to her ultimate fate. The routine of her days that bled into one another, the feeling of time passing by, the defeated notion of watching the world change around her while she stayed in the shadows of her shop as a mere spectator.

Maybe she was destined to merely sell the great works of authors long past and not be a part of their elite community.

She tightened her ponytail, slipped on her shoes which were peeking out from behind a pile of Virginia Woolf's essays, and went downstairs to her bookshop, never once daring to hope that her life was about to magically change.

Chapter II
The Stranger

A rusted hanging bell chimed softly in the corner as Eleanor Driftwood swept into the hallway of her daughter's musty bookshop, a rush of frosty winter air blew in behind her as she closed the wooden door firmly. It seemed each time she came to visit, the door grew heavier and heavier.

The worn sign, 'Bookshop 'Round the Corner' that hung upon a swirling hook outside, rattled like the bones of a deceased playwright. Eleanor shuddered, it felt like something out of a Dickens novel. All that was missing was the ghost of Marley clattering his chains looking for redemption.

Eleanor smiled grimly to herself, maybe Franchesca's penchant for reading dark tales was getting to her, she thought as she rummaged in her purse to check her phone. Her daughter hadn't answered any of her texts and Eleanor doubted whether Franchesca even used the mobile device as anything but a casual paper weight.

"Franchesca?" she called out as she ran a hand through her frosted dark hair. Droplets of dewy snow fell softly to the

13

floor marking her presence.

It was a small shop with a narrow entrance that branched out into a wide circular room crammed from ceiling to floor with built-in shelves and cupboards; shelves and cupboards that were currently overflowing with books ranging from an assortment of subjects and authors and unfortunately arranged just as haphazardly. It looked like an untamed hobbit hole, in her generous opinion.

A hazardous wooden staircase was tucked away in the back of the shop leading up to her daughter's living compartments. Given the usual state of affairs of the place, Eleanor pursed her lips as she imagined the chaotic conditions of Franchesca's room.

"Mum?" A feather duster rose up from the bottom of a shelf in the corner of the room, followed by a pink baseball hat.

"Franchesca?" Eleanor reached out towards her daughter, "Whatever *are* you doing under there? And why are you wearing a hat indoors?"

"Oh this?" Ray lifted her head too abruptly and banged it on the shelf overhead. "Ouch." She lifted her hat half way off and rubbed her temple. Ray turned to her mother, "Hi." She gestured warningly to an old gentleman peering closely at the bookcases, his oversized glasses curiously pressing up against the spines. "I have a customer," she muttered.

"Who? The cat?"

An indignant mewl echoed from the top of the stairs where Ray had given Molly a saucer of milk and some leftover tacos. "Her name is Molly, actually. But good of you to remember her," Ray replied, readjusting her pony tail. "Was there anything else?" she asked airily, twirling the duster expertly in one hand, hoping her voice didn't betray her mounting frustration at her mother's impromptu visit.

"I had a feeling you were mucking about in this shop," Eleanor said with exasperation, her daughter's silent plea to be cordial ignored. "You needn't bother clearing up all your father's clutter," her grey eyes narrowed as she cast a disdainful glance at the books spilling out from the shelves, "He certainly didn't give a damn."

Ray's head snapped up as a retort flew to her lips, a habit she had acquired over the years of her mother snipping at her father. She bit her words back remembering the customer in the shop. And the fact that he was the only customer she had seen in three hours. The lack of revenue and her impending rent forced her to muster a smile. "I enjoy doing it."

Ray turned to the customer who was humming merrily, "So sorry about the disturbance," she said pasting a bright smile on her face, hoping Eleanor would get the hint and perhaps keep her charming remarks to herself.

The gentleman turned to her, his eyes twinkling behind his thick, black-rimmed glasses, "What disturbance?"

Eleanor lay a reassuring hand on her shoulder, "Darling, it's not as though we need the money. Honestly." She cast a disapproving glance at the shelves as though their mere existence challenged her words, "This place is worth more sold and auctioned off than it ever was when your father ran his book keeping business here. Then the books just piled in and it became a shop," she shook her head as though dusting the past years from her memory, "It's probably costing us more to keep it open than it would be to do away with it once and for all."

"Mother," Ray growled.

"It's a matter of fact," Eleanor said with a sniff. Turning to Ray brusquely she continued, "What *have* you done to your hair?" As she lifted Ray's pink baseball cap from her head, a tumble of uncombed dark brown hair cascaded around her shoulders like a glossy, chocolate waterfall. "Much better, although you might want to call Paula for a trim."

Ray tucked her hair back into her hat with a quick twist, "I think I'll let it grow a little more, thanks. I hear eighties hair is making a comeback."

"Not this decade," Eleanor said wryly. She patted her own coiffed-do as she surveyed the surroundings of the shop, her pert nose wrinkled in distaste. "Now don't forget to ring Sophie, she's positively going mad for you to get in touch with her."

Ray shrugged off the twinge of guilt that crept over her; it had been over two weeks since she had visited her mother in London, which meant two weeks away from her best friend, Sophie. And since Ray refused to become a slave to social networking via the world wide web she was more than just a tad cut off from her life back home and, if she admitted it, most of her friends in it.

What was she going to update her friends with anyway? While they were posting pictures of their latest travel escapades, or updating their statuses from 'single' to 'married', Ray was feeling more and more left behind and left wondering why she wasn't doing something wonderful and exciting in her life. And it wasn't that she didn't want to travel. She did. There were so many beautiful places she was positively mad about, Barcelona, New York, Marrakesh, Paris...oh, Paris. She knew she was at the age where your feet positively caught on fire at the thought of exploring the world, and now that she had graduated what was holding her back?

Ray sighed inwardly and looked at the peeling, cream wallpaper where if you looked close enough you could see the ghosts of her childish crayon drawings that her mother had tried to scrub away many years ago. The dark brown carpet had stubborn, blue stains from when she had tried to paint the walls as a little girl. Her whole existence was this shop. And even though she ached to see the world, now was not the time because she couldn't close it down. There was no one else to run it, and somehow Ray couldn't imagine her mother dusting shelves and organizing the book stacks while she was gone. She bit back a little smile at the thought.

A muffled cough caught her attention and broke her reverie, she noticed the elderly gentleman who had come in before Eleanor's snowy entrance. "Mother, I'm actually *quite* busy," she said jerking her head in the direction of the perusing gentleman. She tightened her ponytail, mentally dismissing her guilt at being a social recluse and a not so great friend. Well Sophie was all the way in London, it was technically a long distance relationship, she reassured herself.

"Oh nonsense, darling. Busy doing what?" Eleanor said with a wave of her well-manicured hand, diamonds glittering.

"Busy tending to my customer," Ray bit out each word. What was her mother's problem anyway, couldn't she see that Ray was occupied, albeit with one customer, hopefully a paying one, but still her mother needed to appreciate the fact that she was running an establishment of sorts.

"I don't think the cat counts. Perhaps if you were more social instead of spending all your time in this shop and writing that novel," Eleanor began gently. She carefully removed a stack of books that were balanced precariously on the edge of a chair and sat down. "I suppose it's good you are working, it *is* what adults do," she added as an afterthought.

Ray bristled, "Yes. I *am* aware. I have been working since I was seventeen but thanks for the fortune cookie wisdom."

"I still think you ought to be a bit more social. Go out a little more. Meet new people."

Ray's eyes trailed up to the ceiling, counting each crack in the paint hoping that by the time she had counted twenty, her blood pressure would resume a normal rate and her mother would stop asking her incessant questions.

"Well?"

"Well what?" Ray snapped irritably, she could feel the air growing thick with tension. It was the calm before her mother's verbal storm, one that left emotional wreckage in its wake. She glanced down at the tattered pink cushion on the chair and hoped her mother wouldn't make a passing comment on its dismal state of affairs.

"Well maybe you would have people instead of books filling up your chairs, and friends and proper relationships rather than deceased playwrights and depressed poets taking up your time," Eleanor finished, her perfectly plucked left eyebrow arched imperiously.

Ray groaned. "Oh cue the Russian violinist, Mother." This was an all too familiar conversation she had with Eleanor during every visit and secretly one of the reasons Ray tended to visit less and less each month. Each time Eleanor complained about how withdrawn she had become, so awkward around the people she dragged her off to visit. 'And what would you rather be doing?' her mother would snap at her, 'Being on my own!' Ray would reply, 'Books are not people! Romeo will not sweep through the windows of your flat and confess his undying love to you underneath a bloody balcony' her mother would retort and the vicious cycle would once again continue.

Ray examined her chipped fingernails with interest, avoiding Eleanor's critical gaze, "Was there anything else,?" she asked, resisting the urge to roll her eyes. "I really must tend to my flourishing business."

Eleanor gave her a frosty look, "What business? You parade around this shop as though it's got people coming in left, right and center, with that ridiculous feather duster and twenty year old lopsided bit of paper sticking out of your chest!"

That's it. Her mother had gone too far, Ray thought angrily, "I do not *parade* about here. I actually *live* here. And yes, I need a feather duster, to *dust*. It's environmentally friendly, by the way, unlike that tank you drive. And thirdly," she glared at Eleanor while lovingly covering the object in question, "I love this *lopsided bit of paper*. I made it with Dad. It *means* something to me."

The faded blue piece of cardboard paper, covered in a bit of plastic, held together with lots of tape and a steel pin, was one of Ray's most prized possessions. A happy memory she had with her father, so it was only natural that Eleanor found fault with it.

With the flutter of an eyelid she could always recall with stunning clarity the afternoon her father had helped her make it. They had been filing books when Dave decided that his five year old daughter should have a name tag as well, she was after all, as he fondly put it, his little bookworm assistant. With a carefully cut out piece of cardboard and a colorful mix of felt tip pens, Ray had begun drawing her card when she realized that her name was too long to fit. 'Don't wanna be assistant anymore,' she had pouted. 'How about Ray, then?' her father had suggested with a smile, 'You are indeed my little ray of sunshine.'

And since that day, much to her mother's agitation, Franchesca had responded only to Ray. Everyone had accepted the simple name, except the mother who had christened her. Ray sighed as she lightly fingered the frayed cardboard. Her nametag was falling apart, much like this bookshop, much like her life, she mused. But that thought process would verge on the dramatic and currently she had her mother to do the honors.

"Hmm," Eleanor tapped her booted heel against the stone floor. "When did you eat last?" She turned to a stack of books and lifted a plate with a half-eaten sandwich, "How long has this been sitting here?" Her nose wrinkled in distaste as she examined a soggy piece of lettuce. "A week?"

In two quick steps Ray plucked the offensive sandwich from her mother's disdainful hands, "An hour old," she lied, cramming the rest of the sandwich in her mouth. The taste was a mix of watery vegetables and the distinct hint of expired turkey.

Eleanor eyed her suspiciously as Ray swallowed the remaining bite with a bright smile, "I love turkey."

"The things you'll do to prove a point," Eleanor said with a shake of her head as her eyes scanned the shop for another tell-tale sign of her daughter's dilapidated living conditions. "Franchesca!"

"Mother?" Ray replied in an exaggerated tone.

"You don't have a tree!" she exclaimed. "Or Christmas lights, or even a sprig of mistletoe!"

"Or a partridge?" Ray supplied helpfully, wiping her fingers on the sides of her jeans. "Relax, Mum."

"Well, not to be a bother, but you do realize its Christmas

Eve," she stretched out the word to five syllables.

"Mother, you don't say!" Ray said wide eyed, "And silly me, I thought Santa visited every week and snow storms blessed us all in June."

How could she forget the fact that it was Christmas, it was as impossible as forgetting Dickens penned 'A Christmas Carol' or that her neighbors refused to stop drunken caroling at three in the a.m. Ah yes, how anyone could forget it was Christmas. Where all the rest of the shops were decked out in trees and trimmings and children ran about hand in hand, their cheeks glowing and their eyes bright with the anticipation of Christmas morning, the smell of fresh spiced cake from the baker's next door, the carols the school children sang as they passed her shop, their voices off key and the words all jumbled. It felt like it 'twas the night before Christmas every night in this part of town.

"Well, do you think you'd be able to pop by for Christmas tea, or..." Eleanor's voice trailed off as Ray shook her head.

"Mum, really, I've told you I can't. I've got so much writing to do. And with extended Christmas hours the shop has been busy. Which means!" she gestured wildly around the shop, "So much more cleaning to be done." She felt a twinge of guilt at her mother's crestfallen face. "Really, Mum I should be on one of those shows on television where they tell you off for having such a messy house but then they come and clean it so everyone's happy," she joked weakly.

"Yes, perhaps then I'd see more of you once a week between commercials, rather than thrice a year between holidays."

Ray felt her throat constrict, "Mum. Don't." She turned to the window in an attempt to control the torrid thoughts twisting in her mind.

"Well why the hell not, Franchesca!" Eleanor stood up and stalked over to the window, pointing a furious finger at the dust of snow falling from the sky, "It's snowing! It's Christmas! I believe I have the right to see my child at the very least during this season of love. Surely you must have read about it in one of your books!" she added bitterly.

Through the thick blue curtains Ray could see a flurry of white snow falling from the darkening sky. It wasn't just about Christmas and snow, she thought furiously, "It's also a season of giving!" Ray shot back her face flushing crimson.

"What haven't I given you?" Eleanor put a hand to her chest, her eyes widening in shock, "What haven't I tried to give you that you have blatantly refused to accept!"

"You need to give me space, Mother!"

"You moved the hell out at seventeen, I believe that is giving you space. You choose to live over this abysmal wreck of a bookstore, that is giving you space. You never answer your texts or calls. And might I add," she said pointing her finger at Ray, "That you feel you need to prove something to the world when all you're doing is shutting yourself away, nipped up in this cozy, little arrangement of yours, having all the space in the world without a care for the empty space you left behind." She rose up, her coat swirling angrily about her, "Don't you dare tell me I need to give you space."

Ray felt tears of frustration prickle her eyes, "You don't understand, I need ..."

"Tell me. What don't I understand? What do you need?" Eleanor turned to her daughter as a shadow crossed over her lovely features. "Explain."

"Well if you insist on interrogating me," Ray joked weakly. Why her mother had to make every conversation the grounds for a sweeping battle was beyond her comprehension. If she could just understand that Ray needed her own little space to find her own little place and figure out where she belonged. If her mother would let go of the grudge she had held against her father and realize that the disheveled bookshop was the only place Ray felt at home, where she actually belonged. More than her own home in London did Ray feel the presence of her absent father. Deceased father, she mentally corrected herself. Her father had died when she was but a child of six, her only recollection of him was the musty scent of paper and ink, that magical afternoon they had made her beloved name tag and the one faded photograph framed over the empty fireplace in the shop. That was all. Her mother did not like to talk about him, a fact she had stopped bothering to conceal from Ray over the years. What used to be a flourishing accounting business in his bachelor days became a bookshop after Dave had a family.

All Ray knew of her parent's tumultuous relationship was that her father had spent most of his time in his shop researching and preparing lectures for his University classes. Eleanor, meanwhile, had raised Ray almost single-handedly since birth. After the death of her husband Eleanor had closed up the place abandoning the memories it held, hired a nanny and moved to her parents' grand estate in London.

It was only until the reading of the will that Eleanor

discovered Dave had left the shop to their daughter, a fact she had no desire to act upon until she realized that Ray had inherited the love of books from her father and that it would be cruel to deny her the one thing she cherished above all; her memories with him in the bookshop.

When Ray had been accepted to attend the University of Bath she had opted out of renting a flat and had moved into her father's closed shop. The small studio above the shop where Ray had grown up was all the space she needed. It served wonderfully as a library and above all, a refuge. Though Eleanor had insisted on refurnishing the place, Ray had profusely refused. She loved it the way it was; the way her father had left it.

And now here they were, six years later, arguing over the same thing. Why had Ray left home? Why wasn't she happy? When was she coming back? Why didn't she visit as often? Ray felt her shoulders sag, these really were trying times.

"Well?" Eleanor said.

"Mum, I'd rather not do this when I have company."

"Franchesca Driftwood, your books do not count as guests in my presence," Eleanor snapped impatiently.

Ray looked up, her dark eyes meeting her mother's

identical pair, and she knew her own reflected a stormy grey. "Mum, I literally just finished my research semester and it's already taken me a year to start this bloody novel, the way it's going it might stretch into two years before I have a decent chapter on my hands," she paused for breath, "And secondly, I'm not just mucking about the shop, I love being here. Thirdly," her words came out in a furious flurry, "You know how I feel about Christmas and every other chocolate holiday that comes our way, so really there's no need to celebrate ..."

"I beg your pardon," Eleanor's eyes flashed molten silver. "What did you say?"

"*Eee*," Ray squeaked.

"Don't you *eee* your way out of this," Eleanor continued, "Regardless of what you may think about Christmas, it is still an occasion to be with family and loved ones."

"Pity we need an occasion to mark family days," Ray said her voice thick with bitterness. "What happened to free will?"

"What the devil is that supposed to mean?"

"It means that one should not be obligated to fulfill certain duties based on the date of a Gregorian calendar!" Ray exclaimed. She pulled out a thick book from under the pile on the table and began flipping the pages rapidly, "Mum, look, it

29

clearly says here that Christmas is a pagan holiday. The Romans, quite literally made it up to benefit the..."

"Pagan or not, if it wasn't for Christmas holidays, I don't think I would ever see you," Eleanor said quietly. Her eyes took in her daughter standing in the middle of the crowded room with her worn-out orange shoes, the frayed pink cushion, the shabby carpet and the shelves thick with dust. Franchesca looked like a little rag doll in a little doll house with burdens too heavy for her small shoulders. She wished her daughter would just try to take care of herself a little more. "Just try, Franchesca."

Ray felt a lump in her throat and she swallowed thickly, "I'll try my best," she conceded softly.

Eleanor, a good deal taller than Ray in her high heeled boots, stepped closer and swept her daughter up in an uncharacteristic hug. "Please do, darling."

Ray inhaled the fragrance of her mother's hair and the familiar perfume that clung to her coat and felt tears well up in her eyes, why did they always have to have a falling out in order to hug. "I will."

Eleanor's embrace tightened but the presence of the book distanced her from hugging Ray properly, she looked down at the book pressed against her daughter, "There always seems to be something between us," she said softly, her words falling like silent tears.

Ray looked down at the faded book in her hands and felt her cheeks flame, "Mum, no it's not like that."

"Right then," Eleanor said, her voice business like, "I shall tell Sophie to expect your call tonight and perhaps Paula will be able to book you in for an appointment sometime this week," she affectionately tipped Ray's baseball cap backwards with her finger, "Goodnight, darling."

Ray smiled, "'Night, Mum. Drive safe." She stepped outside to walk her mother to her car, a layer of snow coating her clothes and shoes.

"Go on, get in, it's cold out here," Eleanor chided. "I'll talk to you soon, love. And please keep your mobile on you."

Ray nodded reassuringly and closed the heavy door gently behind her. Where was her phone anyway? Was it even charged? She stood on tiptoes to peek through the peephole to make sure her mother made it to her car without becoming a snowman in the process. When she could hear the rumble of the engine and the retreating screech of tires, Ray leaned her back against the door with a thud. She closed her eyes and

31

exhaled.

Her body slid against the sturdy oak and landed with an unladylike slump that Eleanor would certainly not approve of, on the thick, brown carpet that managed to retain some of its former luster.

Anxious. Her mother's visits always made her anxious. She absently pulled at the fibers of the carpet, a childhood habit. Of course she loved her mother and her mother loved her, but sometimes, Ray thought with a barely suppressed sigh, sometimes she didn't think her mother knew how to love her.

It wasn't as though she wanted to *be* alone; she just wanted to be *left* alone.

Ray sighed and hugged the book close to her chest, her cheek resting atop the leather spine, soft and worn with age. How could she possibly explain that these were more than just pieces of bound paper, they were her everything; her comfort; her refuge; her teachers; her companions; her friends.

She held the book closer, inhaling its familiar scent. It was safe. Safe in here with her books. She really had no one else. Her mother was a two hour drive by car and a three hour ride away by the death trap she liked to call public transport.

Her friends had mostly all disappeared after school and Ray had closed her Facebook account, a form of social suicide she realized. But why would she want to keep in touch with people who merely wrote about how much they missed each other on their walls but never actually bothered to pick up a phone and have a real, genuine conversation. Her phone, she noted as she saw it face down upon a stack of recently paid bills, was an older model of an iPhone. One that most people would be embarrassed to take out of their pockets in the light of day. Picking it up, Ray vowed to charge it more frequently and keep it with her more often than not. Notifications for missed texts, Candy Crush invites and over twenty missed calls greeted her. She groaned and put it back over the bills. It served better as a paper weight.

No, Ray was fed up of the internet and mobile phones and all their ill found glory. All she needed was some more time to fix up the shop and hopefully, if she was lucky enough, make some new friends, she thought looking fondly at a fraying copy of Shelley's Frankenstein.

Desire, revenge, passion, suspense, all found within the pages of a book. Each page a thrill. Each story a destiny fulfilled. She closed her eyes dreamily, why did she need real people when a book was so much more fulfilling?

"I'm sorry if I came at a bad time," a kindly voice jolted her from her reveries.

Ray's eyes flew open and her book fell on the floor with a thud. How could she have forgotten about her customer? "Sir, I do apologize," she said, quickly retrieving the book. "It's the holidays," she added with a rueful smile. That line usually made up for any form of uncomfortable familial behavior. Ray's inquisitive eyes strayed to her customer's faded, brown boots; they were pointed up, almost elfish looking. She quickly straightened up to her full height, curiously regarding the gentleman before her.

He smiled at her, his face crinkling into a collage of wrinkles and lines, "Not to worry, my dear." Clearing his throat awkwardly, he ventured once more, "I couldn't help but overhear that you didn't care for the holidays?"

Ray hesitated at the mild disapproval of his tone. What was she supposed to say, that Christmas was a grand scheme that had little to do with religion and more to do with the commercialism that came along with most holidays? "Well, actually ..."

He held up a wrinkled hand, "Forgive me if I'm intruding.

34

Everyone is entitled to their own beliefs." His long fingers trailed along the spine covers as he continued to peruse the bookshelf.

"No, it's fine," Ray said with a resigned sigh. "No one really wants to hear me vent about what's wrong with it," she let out a little laugh, "Was there anything I could help you with?" It was getting quite late; surely he had somewhere to be. Ray observed him as he examined the shelf, following him past the book stacks, his features suggested that he would have been quite dashing in his youth. But why was he alone? It made her sad to think that such a kindly gentleman had no company.

Get real, Ray, she chided herself. He probably has a house full of grandchildren that look like a Norman Rockwell painting at the dinner table. Satisfied with the story she had made up for her customer, Ray volunteered her services once more, "Was there anything in particular you were looking for, sir?"

"Hmm." He scanned the rows of books with a practiced eye, his long fingers dancing over the volumes, like reeds in the Spring wind. "A riveting adventure or perhaps a romance worthy of the ages. No, no, Greek tragedy, I think. Hmm." The peculiar man turned to Ray, "What would you recommend, Franchesca?"

"Oh, it's Ray actually," she smiled and pointed to her name tag, "Only my mother calls me Franchesca. She never really quite caught onto Ray," she said with a small grin.

"As you prefer," he said with a little bow. "What would you recommend, Ray?"

Ray spread her arms wide, "All of them."

With a chuckle, he walked towards the mantelpiece across the circular room, "There's magic in all of them, is there not?"

She nodded. At least one person understood what she meant, even if he did have questionable footwear.

He continued his slow pace of the room his fingertips flowing along the spines against the walls, "I couldn't help but overhear," he began apologetically.

"Oh no, it's fine," Ray rolled her eyes, "The way me and my mother go at it I'm sure the Irish heard."

"Regardless, I do apologize. But I couldn't help but hear that you wanted to be a writer, yes?" he said with an encouraging smile.

"A starving artist, more like," Ray mumbled. She didn't

want to get into her sob story about how she couldn't write. Not like Austen, not like Bronte, not like Rossetti, not like anyone worth mentioning. "I went to school to be a writer when everyone else went to school to be a lawyer. The way things are progressing I'll probably end up living in a box somewhere scribbling on scraps of junk mail."

His large frame shook merrily under his brown coat as he chuckled. "Right ray of sunshine, aren't you, my dear?"

Ray gave him a sardonic smile, "The weather calls for snow, with an overcast of doom and gloom this evening." Her eyes traveled to the frosted glass peeking through the curtains, it was a beautiful night, the kind of night to share with a loved one tucked in with a book and cup of hot tea. Not the kind of night to be telling your life story to a complete stranger.

She turned to him, feeling his eyes observing her, "Perhaps all the great stories have already been told," she said shoving her hands in her jeans pockets.

He cocked his head to the side, "Do you really believe that, Ray?" his hand momentarily ceased its journey across one end of the shelf to the other.

"I don't know, maybe?"

"The greatest tale ever told, is the one you have yet to write," he said his voice suddenly serious. He beckoned towards her to come from the window and join him. His deft hands plucked a book from the middle of the shelf. He handed it to her, "For you."Ray drew her dark eyebrows together curiously and looking up at him first, then at the book that lay heavily in her hands. It was unlike ones she had seen in the shop, which usually wouldn't have been surprising with the amount of books that were seeping from every nook and cranny. But this one was different. There were no trails of dust coating the cover, no title or author engraved in worn print. The cover itself was intriguing; she trailed her fingers over the royal blue velvet. Perhaps it was just a fancy jacket for a more familiar story inside, she thought, opening it. It was completely blank, she ruffled through the pages, the cream colored paper was clear of type or ink. "It's beautiful."

"It's yours," he replied with a smile twinkling behind his spectacles.

"Strange how I've never come across it before," Ray mused once more studying it. "It looks like a journal, I'm sure someone must have left it behind, or something."

"Well it's in your shop, on your bookshelf, I believe it's

yours by way of deduction," he nodded with an air of certainty that Ray didn't question further. Before she could open her mouth to ask him once more if he needed anything, the shrill ring of the telephone upstairs cut through her thoughts.

"I'll be right back," she said apologetically, the book clasped securely in her hands. Funny, it had felt as heavy as an encyclopedia just a moment ago, now it felt feather light like a book of poems. Strange. She sprinted towards the staircase at the back of the shop as the piercing ringing of the phone continued. "Please make yourself comfortable," she gestured to her cozy armchair in the corner beside a lamp. Hopefully he wouldn't mind the tattered pink cushion.

"I'll be fine, Ray. You take care, now," he said as he wrapped himself in his coat, "And remember..."

She turned halfway from the stairs, her eyes searching for his figure, "Sir?" Where had he gone? She craned her neck, peering anxiously from the stairs, "Hello?"

Silence.

"The greatest tale that has yet to be told is the one you have yet to write," came the whisper of the gentleman close to Ray's ear. She shrieked at the nearness of his voice. She could have sworn she had seen his shadow by the front door a moment ago. There was a distinctive clang of a saucer being overturned and Molly's high pitched mewl. Stumbling on the stairs, she tried to regain her balance but her shoes were still wet with snow from when she had walked her mother out to the car. With a cry she fell, the world slipping under her feet.

The man's words echoed in Ray's ear, and as she closed her eyes and fell into a never ending abyss, her thoughts grew heavy and dim like a room that is suddenly left dark after a candle is burnt out. It never occurred to her that her mother hadn't been able to see the stranger in her shop.

Chapter III
Knight Errant

She was still breathing. *Good.* That was always a promising sign of life, Ray thought gingerly turning her head from side to side. She heard a sharp crack and felt an acute pain between her shoulder blades. *Bad.* That was a bad sign. Her body was hurting in places she never knew existed with a pain so excruciating she had to cover her mouth to keep from screaming. She didn't feel trickles of blood oozing out of her skin, so she wasn't cut. Just surface injuries. But the pain...she couldn't recall the last time she had fallen so hard, or hurt so much. *Just breathe.* Her hands fell back to the ground as she lay her head back on the soft earth, inhaling the scent of dewy grass...g*rass?*

Ray's eyes flew open and with a groan she sat up half way and surveyed her surroundings. *Where was she?* Rolling green meadows greeted her, the soft whisper of a breeze tickled her hair, the fragrance of wild flowers wafted in the air and she knew she wasn't in the bookshop anymore. In fact she didn't think she was in England anymore. At least not in the South

West End.

"I must've hit my head harder than I thought," she murmured, easing herself in a sitting position.

"Yeah, you didn't look too thrilled when you landed either," came a deep, male voice from behind Ray.

She let out a little yelp of surprise and stood up on wobbly feet. She hadn't seen anyone. *Was she starting to hear things?* Turning around quickly Ray lost her balance and slipped.

"Steady." A pair of strong hands smoothly held her before she collapsed on the ground again. "That was a quite a fall."

Her wide gray eyes met the most astonishing pair of green and Ray felt her heart skip a beat. She was looking into the most handsome face the depths of her wildest imagination could have conjured. Not conventionally handsome like that of a tanned life guard, but rather classically handsome, like that of a statue of a long forgotten Greek god or a story book prince brought to life.

Though he was just dressed just like an ordinary boy, she thought surveying his dark blue jeans, black cardigan sweater hanging loosely over a gray t-shirt, something in his manner; the way he held himself told Ray that there was nothing at all ordinary about him. He couldn't be more than twenty five. His lips were curved up in a cross between a mocking smile and a smirk as though he could sense why she seemed flustered. His jaw was cut and well defined with just a hint of a 5 o' clock shadow, his nose was strong and narrow, and his eyes, those eyes that were cutting into her own took her breath away.

Or maybe, a reasonable voice interjected, that was just the fall talking and she was hallucinating his good looks.

Ray swallowed thickly, hoping he couldn't hear the thundering beat of her heart as she brushed his hand away, "I'm fine." Her breath caught once more as he raised a hand to cup her cheek, his eyes searching hers, "Are you quite sure?"

Ray nodded. "Mmhmm," she said in what she hoped was a casual voice, but came out high pitched and strangled. She quickly cleared her throat. Really, propriety and enough late night specials had taught her better than to fall for complete strangers, quite literally, she thought with a wince as her head began to pound mercilessly.

He smiled crookedly, his white teeth flashing. "Sure?"

Ray looked up, "No, not really," she admitted with a nervous laugh. *God, why did she sound like such a moron?* He was just attractive, it wasn't as though she had to lose all her mental faculties in one fatal swoop. Bad enough he had seen her fall and stumble twice.

He leaned down gallantly, "I'm here to help you," he said offering her his arm once more.

Ray tentatively reached out her hand to accept his offer, but thought better of it and pulled away suspiciously. "Why?"

One moment he was looking at her in confusion and the next he laughed; a deep, rich sound that sounded like a warm fire on a frosty day.

Ray scowled as he looked down at her like she was an endless source of amusement, "Because Dorothy, you're not in Kansas anymore and I think you could use the company."

"I'm quite fine on my own, thank you," Ray said waspishly, pushing her bangs out of her eyes. To her ears her remark sounded childish but here she was in a strange and beautiful place, with a strange and beautiful boy; and if it wasn't a dream and if she wasn't dead, it didn't make any sense.

"Is that right?" he smirked crossing his arms over his wide chest.

"Uh, yeah," Ray said. She couldn't trust her own eyes, let alone a completely gorgeous stranger who was offering her his help. Ray lifted her chin, "I'm quite alright, thanks. I'll just be on my way now."

"And where do you plan on going?" he asked sardonically, his voice laced with amusement.

Ray turned to glare at him as she lifted herself up from the grass, as awkward and unsteady as a new born deer, "Home, thank you." She couldn't be that far from the town center, she must've somehow sleepwalked or something, to the outskirts of the city and wandered in the country somewhere. Yes. That sounded about right. She was in the country somewhere. "I can't be too far from Somerset," she reasoned aloud, hoping that her voice didn't betray her sense of distrust of the entire situation.

The curious boy put a hand on her shoulder and said in a grave voice, "Somerset is but a memory now."

"What?"

"I'm sorry, you can't go home," he repeated, his eyes crystal clear, void of any traces of humor.

"Oh my God!" Ray held her hands to her throat, "Am I dead?" Waves of panic washed over her. *That had to be it!* She had died somehow when she had fallen. Her mother had always told her that her father's books would be the end of her. It was after that strange man had left. *Yes.* Maybe he killed her? *No.* Surely she would've had some recollection of her own murder. She absently looked down at her orange shoes, funny she always thought that people were barefoot in white, flowing gowns and all ethereal like in Paradise. Yet she felt clumsy as ever, stumbling over her feet and tripping over her words.

"Did I die?" she whispered.

"What?"

"Am I dead?!" she shrieked. A mother bird chirped indignantly in the distance. Why wasn't he saying anything when even birds seemed to have an opinion? "Did I die? Are we in Heaven?" She paused and looked at him as though she was seeing him for the first time. Suddenly his beauty made perfect sense.

She swallowed thickly, reaching out to touch his face "Are you an angel?"

"In jeans?"

"Doesn't matter," she said breathlessly. Somehow she had made it to Paradise, perhaps she hadn't been as terrible to her mother as she thought she had been. She exhaled, that was a relief. It was also a relief to know that Heaven and a Garden of

Eden truly existed.

"I don't even remember dying, I guess it must have been a pretty bad fall," she said conversationally, tucking her wayward hand in her pocket. Even if he was an angel that didn't mean she could just grab his face. There were probably rules here about these sorts of things. Honestly. Weren't people supposed to be better versed in Heaven? If not a little more savvy when it came to the opposite sex.

He pinched the bridge of his nose and exhaled. "No you did not die, Franchesca."

Franchesca. Her name rolled off his tongue, sending unexpected shivers of delight through Ray. It was a new sensation, unfamiliarly delicious.

"I beg your pardon?"

"Franchesca," he smiled slowly, observing her.

And once more the feel of her name on his lips sounded so lush and foreign, for a moment Ray couldn't grasp that he was talking to her. Feeling betrayed by her reaction to this mocking young man she narrowed her eyes at him, "How do you know my name?" she demanded.

He pointed at her chest, "It's on your name tag."

She looked down at her dismal name tag, fraying around

47

the edges, "Actually, it says Ray," she pointed out with a superior smile.

"Well, Ray usually tends to be the shortened form of that name."

"No, it doesn't."

"Yeah, but it does."

"No."

"Isn't yours?"

"Well, yes but -"

"Didn't you know that?"

"Of course *I* knew that," she said exasperated. "The question is how did you?"

"Because it's the shortened form of such a name," he concluded matter-of-factly with a boyish grin.

Ray couldn't help but feel that she was on the losing end of the conversation, "Aren't you clever, Mr. Holmes," she muttered under her breath. She folded her arms across her chest, covering her name tag and all other possibly revealing parts of herself from his gaze and glared at him. "You know, I don't even know your name, and since you don't come with a name tag, it's only polite that you tell me yours."

"James."

James. She liked the sound of it. "I see," she responded curtly. "Well, *James*, if this isn't Heaven and I'm not dead, then would you be so kind to let me in on what's going on?"

"Trust me, you're quite alive. I believe a sound temperament is required to frolic about with angels in Paradise," he added with a smirk.

The nerve. "I'm quite sound!"

He turned back to Ray and raised a mocking eyebrow, "Clearly."

"Ok genius, where are we then?" Ray walked behind him, every two strides of hers matching one of his own. She wasn't used to feeling so helpless and unsure in any situation and she didn't like it in the least. "Where are we?" she repeated.

Indifferent to her turbulent thoughts, James strolled casually along the edge of the sparkling lake and inhaled deeply, avoiding her question. "Gorgeous, isn't it?" he breathed tilting his head back.

Ray narrowed her eyes staring at his silhouette against the light of the sun. He really was tall. *Over six feet?* Easily. *Stunning?* Without a doubt. The scenic view wasn't bad either, Ray thought scanning the horizon. It looked like something out of an Andersen fairy tale. No wonder she felt that she didn't quite fit in. She cleared her throat, "Commenting upon the view will not evade my persistency." "I just want you to take a moment and admire it," he said. He held out his hand to her, "Come."

Ray frowned in suspicion, "Where?"

"Here." And in one fluid movement he had pulled her up to the edge of the lake, the toes of her shoes hanging perilously. A smile played upon his lips as she squealed in surprise and dropped her book on the grass beside her, "Could you for one moment allow yourself to enjoy where you are and not question why you're here."

Ray's lips formed a retort as her eyes narrowed at him, but his own were closed as the sun basked his upturned face with light. Once more Ray couldn't help but stare in awe at the perfection of his well-defined jaw and the serene expression his face wore when he wasn't aggravating her. Enjoy herself? Well, why not. She closed her eyes and inhaled deeply allowing the sweet breeze to play through her hair, her hat left behind in some other world she must have crossed to be here. "It's like a dream," she whispered. Without thinking of what she was doing her body leaned forward, drawn to the intoxicating blend of sunshine and air. "Eee!"

"Careful!" A pair of familiar hands pulled her down backwards onto the grass.

She landed hard on the ground and glared at him, "Was all that force really necessary?"

"Would you rather be drowning?" he shot back.

"It couldn't have been that deep," she said lifting her chin to peer over into the lake once more. The silvery blue depths shimmered invitingly, "It's just a lake." Honestly, it wasn't as though he had saved her life or anything dramatic like that. She knew how to swim.

"Says the girl who's never been here before," he smirked. "Got a little carried away there, didn't you? I best be on the lookout if you're a wild child." He paused, "Then again, considering when we are, you'll most likely be preoccupied with..."

What? "I beg your pardon, *when* we are?" she repeated dubiously. Peering closer at him, she reached up and laid her palm on his forehead, "Are you feeling quite alright, you seemed articulate enough when you were telling me off a moment ago, but I do believe you said *when* we are."

He smiled and caught her small hand in his much larger one, "When."

51

Was he mental? Ray pulled her hand back, "What do you mean *when*?"

"Well, does this look like present day England to you, Franchesca?" he nudged her gently with his shoulder. "We traveled in time."

"Wait! Just wait a minute," Ray stood up shakily, her feet wobbling to regain her sense of time and balance. And sanity. "You mean to tell me we've somehow stumbled through time and ...? What?" she glared at the boy standing in front of her looking positively tickled "What is so funny?" she demanded, her hands on her hips.

"You honestly mean to tell me, you have no idea where we are?" he said, all seriousness once more.

"I'm sorry do you come with a map and private tour?" Ray said in a scornful voice. *What was he being so clever for anyway, it's not as if he was in charge, he just put himself there.* "Well?" she raised her eyebrow.

"I come with a great many benefits," James said suggestively winking at Ray who rolled her eyes, "That are limited, unfortunately for you, to personalized walking tours and the occasional ironic remark."

"Ok, so clearly you don't know what you're talking

about," Ray said, gathering herself, "I'm just going to have to figure this out on my own."

"You really don't have to," he said quietly, "On your own, I mean."

She looked at him darkly, "Look, I know you mean well and that you're probably just a really nice guy, but this has to be a trick of sorts. A dream or something. A mirage maybe." her voice faltered, as her gaze swept the rolling hills that stretched to the horizon. "Right?"

In a lightning quick movement James turned her hand and pressed a hot kiss on the inside of her wrist.

Her breath caught as his lips seared her skin. She turned to him wordlessly, her dark eyes wide.

"Feel that?"

She opened her mouth ready to say something clever, something witty, something indignant but nothing but a high pitched peep escaped her lips.

"Well squeaking is better than what you were doing a moment ago," he smiled, green eyes flashing mischief.

"And what was that?" Ray asked, her voice returning to her. She folded her arms firmly over her chest and glared at him, refusing to be swept away like some damsel in distress in some cheap, 50p romance at yard sales with over-the-top covers. Her left eyebrow arched imperiously and she had the suspicious feeling she was sounding a lot like her mother at the moment, "Well?"

"We traveled," he said matter-of-factly.

"Oh right, yes we traveled. That's what people *do*, James, you know when one foot moves in front of the other."

"We traveled, Franchesca," he began once again, enunciating each word. "Through time. Time traveled."

"Time traveled?" Ray sputtered. "What are we, trapped in some sort of BBC special?" she scoffed. "Spare me the details and just say we're lost in some strange, unknown part of town that may or may not have a large Mormon population. You should really ask for directions."

"There aren't any Mormons here, not to my recollection," he said conversationally to Ray. "There's only one direction we're supposed to go." Gesturing before him he smiled back at her, "Well come on. What are you waiting for?"

"Someone with a sense of direction," she muttered under her breath, but she reluctantly fell into step with him.

Hastily, Ray cleared her throat, "Well, I'll be on my way, now."

"Oh, yeah? Where exactly do you plan on going?" he said with a quirk of his eyebrow.

It wasn't as though she had anywhere else to go and though she would refuse to admit it he did seem quite familiar with their surroundings, strange as his reasoning was, she didn't think they were completely lost. She bent down to gather her dropped book and held it to her chest. It felt familiar and comforting, the only tangible object from her own time she could trust in this strange place. "*Just* so you know I'm not following you. You simply *happen* to be walking in front of me."

He chuckled softly, "Sure."

They walked along the beaten down lane where silver blue butterflies wove in and out of the tall grass, the only sound was Ray's shoes giving out an occasional squeak of protest. She hoped they wouldn't give way and turn to a pile of orange mush with laces. James seemed like the kind of person who would either insist on carrying her or giving her his own footwear. Either way, she grudgingly admitted, he was a gentleman.

An oddly quiet gentleman considering how vocal he had been earlier. Ray cleared her throat, trying to get his attention.

James didn't look back at her. She faked a small cough and the only response was the soft, rustling breeze. Ray tightened her ponytail and tore off a long blade of grass and waved it in front of her, "Hey."

"Hi."

"I can't remember the last time I've walked so much," she said with a small smile, looking up at him. Nothing was worse than making small talk, but at least they were having a conversation and perhaps she could get a few more substantial answers out of him.

"Don't get out much?" he asked over his shoulder.

"Not really, actually. I always mean to go out, it just doesn't happen as often as I'd like, I guess," her voice trailed off. When was the last time she had actually been outside for a walk? Obviously not for some time, her legs were already aching and her feet sore.

"You alright?" James stopped and faced her. "We can stop if you want."

"No, I should be fine," Ray said lifting her chin. "These shoes were made for walking and that's just what they'll do."

His eyes trailed down from her flushed cheeks to her dilapidated shoes and smirked.

"Shut up."

"I didn't say anything!" he laughed.

"I know what you're thinking."

"Highly doubtful," he crossed his arms over the expanse of his chest and leaned closer to her, "Highly. Doubtful."

Ray felt her heart skip a beat. Or two. Or three. She really wasn't used to being so close to someone so infuriating and attractive. Someone who may be flirting with her.

"What's your last name?" she asked casually.

"Why?" She could hear the amusement in his voice, as though he knew where the conversation was heading.

"I want to Google you and make sure you aren't a wanted felon."

James stopped abruptly and tilted his head to one side, looking at Ray quizzically, "Are you always this suspicious of people?"

Yes. "No."

"You're a terrible liar," he chuckled.

"Ok, think of this from my point of view," Ray said, pushing her bangs from her eyes. "One moment I'm in my shop in snowy England and the next I'm here in this endless summer. With you."

"With me."

"Yes James, with you."

"So what's the problem?"

He couldn't be serious. Ray searched his expression for signs of humor but he seemed to be utterly sincere. "So this is your thing, then? This is what you do? You just appear out of nowhere to save people?"

"Something like that," James said with a trace of a smile. "You are by far the most entertaining of them all."

Ray scowled.

"And the fairest."

"Highly doubtful," Ray muttered. Now he was definitely mocking her. There was nothing extraordinary about her. She knew that. She was barely average height. Her weight ranged from a UK 6 to 10 depending on how motivated she was to go grocery shopping. Her skin once a light olive was now pale from the many hours spent in the shop. One of her middle school teachers had told her she could never be a politician because every thought was apparent on her face. Well it wasn't her fault her face betrayed her shock at the lack of her teacher's knowledge of geographic cities. She supposed her only lovely feature was her hair but it's not as if she had to do anything with it, it just grew.

Her shoulders slumped a little and she exhaled softy. No, Ray wasn't anything special, he was definitely mocking her.

A pair of warm hands tilted her chin up to the sunlight. "What's wrong?" James asked gently, his thumb caressing her cheek.

"Nothing," Ray shrugged away from his touch.

"You don't believe me?"

"I don't care." She swallowed thickly and looked at the radiant sun, shielding her eyes so he wouldn't see the defeated expression on her face.

"If you could only see what I see," he whispered softly.

"I hope what you're seeing is a way out here," Ray lied stomping ahead of him into a shaded clearing where a large weeping willow stood, her drooped branches swaying to nature's silent melody. Where could they possibly be? Some unexplored part of England, perhaps? But if James was telling the truth and they had stumbled through Time together, then maybe, just maybe they were in a little slice of Paradise untouched by man.

"Still think I'm wanted in seven different continents?" James whispered in her ear.

Ray shivered at the warmth of his voice so close to her, "Maybe." She looked up at him, her cheeks coloring. For all the squabbling she had done since they met she still had no idea what his last name was. Or what he was actually doing here with her. "I'm sorry you don't come with a name tag."

James leaned against the bark of the tree, his face partially shrouded by the slow, swinging branches. "Still curious?"

Ray nodded, her eyes fixed on his.

"Still going to try and look me up on the internet?"

"Definitely."

"With what phone?" he asked with a smirk.

Damnit. "Oh don't you worry," Ray said with as much confidence as she could muster, "I have my phone right here," she tapped the back of her jeans pocket with her left hand. "Right here," she smacked the back of her jeans harder. "Good ol' mobile which I have right here."

"Yeah, but you don't."

"How do you know?"

"I would have noticed. Secondly you don't seem like the kind of person who cares much about technology," he said with a nonchalant shrug.

"Firstly, *you* can relax. What do you mean you would have noticed? And secondly what do you mean I don't seem like I care about technology?"

James folded his arms across his chest and exhaled as though he was getting ready to give a rousing speech. Ray held up her hand to stop him, sat down on a grassy stump by the tree and gestured for him to continue.

He raised an eyebrow, "Comfortable?"

Ray wiggled on her seat. "Very. Please enlighten me."

James turned his neck from side to side, a definitive crack resounding, before he began, "If you had a mobile on you, you would have either broken it during your crash landing or whipped it out immediately to find reception and call someone. Since you did neither, I safely assumed you weren't carrying an electronic device. Nor did you ask whether this place had any reception or where the closest free Wi-Fi was available. Also we have been walking for more than twenty minutes, studies have shown that people in uncomfortable situations tend to whip out their mobile devices at least once every three minutes, if only to avoid conversation. You don't fidget or get agitated when confronted with new situations which suggests that you lead an isolated life with minimal social interaction. And since you can't stop thinking out loud, which I find refreshing for a change, I know that you aren't used to not knowing answers or not being in full control of situations." He paused, "Personally I was a little offended that you didn't ask for my Instagram, but that was before I concluded you didn't have your mobile with you. So please, continue to smack your bum all you like, if only for my amusement."

Ray could feel her mouth open and close like the pet goldfish she once had as a child. No words came out. His observations of her mannerisms were beyond anything she had expected. They had only just met but he seemed to know so much about her just by watching her. She bit her lip. He seemed to know her better than Sophie, better than her own mother.

"Well?"

"Well I won't be smacking my bum. You seem to like it too much."

"Pity." He reached down and held out his hand to Ray helping her up from where she was rooted on the ground, still in a slight bout of aftershock after his speech.

She looked up at him, hesitating only slightly before she

placed her hand in his.

"Still thinking of calling the police?" he winked, as he tucked her right hand into his left one.

"Not when you've got me red handed," Ray joked nervously. Why was he holding her hand like she was some wayward child? Or did it mean something more? Or was he making silent observations at how tightly she was holding onto his hand? She could just imagine what he would say, 'Evidently Franchesca, you have issues with abandonment dually noted by the way you clasp my hand.' Or was he simply just making sure she wouldn't run away before he sacrificed her to forest demons?

"So, James?" she asked in what she hoped was a casual tone.

"Yes, Franchesca?"

"So you're really not like, a serial killer are you?"

"I don't think so."

Don't think so? "That's good to know," Ray squeaked.

They continued walking along down the path towards a grassy opening in the forest ahead. Patches of sunlight winked through the branches of sturdy oak trees and if Ray squinted high enough, she could see heads of birds peeking through the foliage. She took a deep breath it really was beautiful here, the air so crisp, so clean it was delicious. It felt like she was breathing in a rainbow of goodness each time she inhaled.

"You know you can talk," James said, "You couldn't seem to stop just a moment ago. I'm a pretty good listener."

"Talk to you about what?" Ray asked narrowing her eyes. After his little show and tell earlier she wasn't sure if she wanted to let him anywhere hear her thoughts.

"Anything. Nothing. I don't mind."

"I don't really have anything to say."

"Somehow I doubt that's true.

"What do you mean?"

"A girl like you seems like she has plenty to say."

"I don't need a psychiatrist. I'm not mental," Ray said stubbornly, her gaze cutting into his. "I don't need you to tell me how to feel, or what to feel, or lie and tell me that there really is a silver lining and that everything will be fine."

James observed Ray carefully as she once again misinterpreted his words. "Then what would you like me to be?"

What? Ray's eyes snapped up, "What do you mean?" *Was this a trick question?*

"What would you like to me to be? How would you like me to help you?" he asked patiently.

Between James and potentially meeting a hitchhiker, Ray really didn't have a stack of options left. But there was something odd about the way he was so obliging. So ready to help Ray. So willing. So genuine. So obvious that there had to be a catch. She gave him a scrutinizing sideways glance, "What do you mean how would I like you to help me?"

James held up his hand, "Whatever you like. I can be your friend. I can be your PhD qualified psychiatrist who quotes Freud every two minutes. Whatever you feel you need, Franchesca."

Ray shrugged helplessly. "I don't know. Like ..." her voice trailed off as she looked about the woods for a glimmer of inspiration. *What did she need? A therapist? Or a friend? Maybe a friendly therapist?* She sighed and felt her shoulders droop wearily. In her mind's eye she retreated to the only safe place she knew for a burst of inspiration. All she saw were shelves and shelves of books, maybe they could talk Shakespeare instead of Freud. If she concentrated enough she could recall the last stack she had been shelving away. It had begun in a haphazard pile on the floor, almost up to the window, where a rare copy of Don Quixote leaned against the wall, majestically, his amour glittering in the sunlit glow of the room. There he was, Don Quixote heading towards the fire breathing windmill while Sancho Panza waves his arms furtively attempting to stop him, to talk sense into him, to save him. A light went on in Ray's mind as she turned to James, "I want you to be my Sancho Panza," she said.

A slow smile spread across his face, radiant as the dawn she had seen this morning, "Sounds like a plan."

Really? Ray peeked at him through her bangs. "Really?"

"Really." He affirmed

"You're willing to be my companion throughout all this chaotic madness in my mind," Ray asked, pointing to her head, "Are you sure?"

"Yeah."

"Cool. I'll let you know if I see a windmill," she said.

"Or a dragon," he teased.

They continued walking in a comfortable silence. "Nice book," James said conversationally, breaking Ray from her thoughts. He nodded towards it.

"Thank you," Ray replied distractedly, handing it to him.

"Looks a little bit plain with no title. I have something

even better for you," the blue felt book that Ray held just a moment ago, transformed into a creamy beige novel with a bright cover. "Meet Arabella," he said grandly replacing the book in Ray's hands.

Her eyes widened in awe and she stared at the new book now resting upon her fingertips, "James, how did you...?" It was like a magic Ray had never seen beyond TV specials. "How?"

"Meet Arabella," he repeated with a smile.

"James, what was..."

"Just go with it," he winked.

"Well, hello," Ray said, pretending to shake hands with the figure on the front, "What damage have you caused the literary world with your heartache?" *Hmm.* "The Female Quixote," she read aloud, "By Charlotte Lennox," she looked up at James, "Can't say I've heard of this, is it something like Don Quixote?"

"Slightly. She's ruled by her imagination, like Don Quixote. Extremely creative, her mind tripping from one possibility to the next."

"I like her already." The cover of her once blue book portrayed a woman, whose features must have been regarded as the epitome of beauty in the eighteenth century, looked demurely to her side, dressed in blue silk garments and modeling a turban on her head. She looked like something out of Sinbad. Ray shook her head in amusement "This is what you're comparing me to?" she asked, raising an eyebrow.

"Perhaps not comparing exactly, but fending you from becoming," James said carefully.

"Why? What's her story? Does she long for adventure and love and romance and ends up going mental because it doesn't exist?" She pursed her lips as she studied the book. Trust James to find the perfect book for her situation.

"This is the story of Arabella, who, under the influence of French romances, seeks to find adventure and love in the most unlikely situations, fusing her life with a flair for the dramatic in order to create the illusion of a fairy tale romance that she longs for," James grinned, "She's a wonderful, beautiful character. I'm sure you'll like her."

"She sounds just peachy," Ray rolled her eyes, but curiosity held her interest. She looked at the heroine on the cover once more, her fingertip tracing the outline of the figure. For a moment she saw her own face reflected in that of the drawing and she blinked twice to clear the image from her eyes. Maybe there was truth in what James was saying and she was destined to meet her literary counterpart once more fluttering in the pages of a romance that could never come to life.

"She reminds me of you, a little," James smiled. "She's quite, quite impulsive. Very emotional. Terribly endearing. And fancies her life were one of the faded romance novels her mother used to read."

He thought she was terribly endearing? Ray was torn between amusement and annoyance. "So basically, she's an idiot," she concluded with a bright smile.

"No, no! Not at all, Franchesca," James rolled his eyes, clearly displeased at her misinterpretation. "She's not. The author's intent was to make readers, especially female readers, aware of the dangers of regarding one's own life as a Romance, with a capital R. Art may imitate life, but life should not always imitate art. Young girls grow up hoping to be Juliet, young men hoping to be a dashing knight errant. It's much too much. The expectations are ludicrous and impossible to live up to," he paused, allowing Ray the time to digest his words, "Do you understand?"

"I'm not trying to be the female lead protagonist," Ray

replied, somewhat miffed. *Did he think she was mental?* Well, besides the painfully obvious fact that they had somehow managed to wind up somewhere in time. Ray wasn't about to live out her life like a book, like a fairy tale. She wasn't. She wasn't the lead character. If anything she'd be an extra, a stage hand, one of the people in the background selling apples. She wasn't the heroine. Not even in her own life story. "I understand perfectly, thank you."

Bemused by Ray's interpretation of his meaning, James attempted once more to drive his point home, "You *are* the female lead protagonist, Franchesca. But this story, *your* story, has an ending only you can create for yourself, it won't be found in the pages of these books," he ticked off a list on his fingers, "Diderot, Buchner, Voltaire, Byron, Balzac. Use these writers as a guide, as a reference, not as an end to all means, but the helpful means to an end," his voice was gentle, yet firm. "You have to realize that now, before you read anything, you have to know that it is a story. Someone's wish fulfillment perhaps. The characters may seem true to life, but they are not real. Everything is made up, fiction, a fairy tale to some degree. Its words put to magic and a story is woven with structure and plot and ..."

"But how can people talk about such emotion if they haven't lived through it?" Ray interjected. Hot blood coursed through her, indignantly, angrily. She felt that she had to defend the Juliet's, the knights-errant and their creators.

"How can you just belittle the words and lives of the poets who toiled their days away penning the perfect sonnet trying to capture a moment in time? It was real to someone. And years later, if someone finds truth and meaning in that very same sonnet, how can that not be true, or just as real?" Her hands trembled with emotion and her arms enveloped around her shoulders in a hug, keeping herself together, keeping herself in check, "It's true though. It's the human condition, that sameness, that closeness that allows us to relate to situations and people and experiences. And whether it's a film, or a sonnet, or a song or a novel, if we can relate to it in some way, in any way, then we're not alone," she leaned forward earnestly, her voice catching, "We're not alone then. So why is it bad if art imitates life and vice versa?" Her shoes scuffed against the grass and she kicked a stray stone ahead, exhausted by her tirade of emotion. What was she trying to defend, anyway? The right to imagination? Surely James was an advocate of such a precious prerogative. No, there was

71

something else he wasn't telling her or something that Ray simply wasn't able to comprehend. *What, though?*

"Here, allow me," James reached over and plucked Ray's book from her hands. Somehow as if by magic, the cover seemed to shimmer and change in front of her very eyes and the encryption read, 'Rousseau, Reveries of a Solitary Walker', written boldly on the front where Arabella in her feather hat had proudly stood.

He skimmed through the pages, frowning until he got to the part he was looking for, clearing his throat and read aloud, "Let me decide my opinions and principles once and for all, and then let me remain for the rest of my life what mature consideration tells me I should be." Laying the book gently back in Ray's hand, he looked at her, "Do you understand?"

"Yes. That we have to make up our own minds and that these books are a guide to helping us find the answers. But, that doesn't mean it's just a story. It doesn't mean it couldn't happen," she crossed her arms stubbornly over her chest. She felt childish, she knew she was acting childish, but James was asking her to give up her hopes and dreams all in one fatal swoop. She cleared her throat, "Isn't the power of imagination the greatest adventure of them all?"

"Franchesca, the power of imagination is both liberating and confining. It can take you places you never thought possible, but it can also trap you to believe in things that may never happen," his eyes looked aged with sorrow, "I'm not telling you to give up everything, and I'm most certainly not suggesting that you stop being who you are. Don't."

Ray tightened her ponytail, a habit that seemed to calm her down when faced with perplexing situations. "Then what are you trying to say, because it feels like I'm doing everything wrong."

"You're doing nothing wrong, but the danger that can come with such a strong belief in the work of fiction, well, surely you can see the perils it could potentially cause."

Rays' eyes flickered to the book in her hands and scrutinized the figure on the front. Her book looked like a three dimensional sticker that children got out of sweet packets. When she turned it at one angle she could see Voltaire's solitary walker treading among fallen leaves. When it was tiled another way, she saw Arabella standing proudly, her lust for adventure shining from her eyes.

"You say it all, with such authority, as though," she paused as the impossible words formed on her tongue, "As though you've been there before, but that's impossible," she finished. "James, you can't know these things."

"Would you rather I show you what I mean?" he asked, his green eyes melting into hers, alight with promise.

Impossible. None of this was possible or real. "What do you mean?" she said hesitantly.

"Let me show you," he repeated.

Ray bit her lip, and put her hand into his own. *Thrills.* It was more than his promise to show her. His touch sent thrills through her. She willed herself not to turn to jelly, to be somewhat calm and collected. "Show me what?" Ray asked in what she hoped was a casual manner. She buffed her nails against her shirt. "Hmm?"

His next words took her breath away.

"I hear you like Jane Austen."

Chapter IV
Finding Jane

The stars twinkled like uncut diamonds in the thick blanket of the night sky as the hues of the setting pink sun began to fade into blue. The faded sounds of stirring human life could be heard close by as an occasional whinny of a horse rang out. The air was unseasonably cool and carried a faint trace of apple blossoms. Ray found herself walking closer to James, they weren't quite touching but his presence alone was comforting in this strange place. And he was warm.

They had been walking for what seemed like an hour or two but something had changed in that time, Ray couldn't quite put her finger on it or explain what it was beyond metaphysical terms, but the aura of the place had shifted as though she were moving from dream to dream in waking sleep.

James seemed to have taken them through the forest to the outskirts of a city. She had felt the grass beneath her feet slowly thin into gravel and then smooth, wet pebbles. They were on the edge of a misty clearing, shrouded by swaying tree branches. The air was spiced with anticipation. He turned to her, his eyes dark emeralds, "Ready?"

For what? Ray nodded, breathless.

He pulled back the graceful branches of a weeping willow obstructing her view and once more Ray felt herself slip through time into another world.

It was England, but it wasn't the England that Ray knew. It was the England she had read about a thousand times for a thousand nights. The England that was described in history books and preserved in encyclopaedias and documented in black and white TV specials. The England she had always dreamed to be a part of had somehow come to life in front of her very eyes. The hustle and bustle of people on horses and wagons wasn't what she had been expecting at all. It didn't smell as smoggy or as industrialized as the revolution that was occurring, but rather earthy like wild flowers and dewy grass.

Men in smart top hats arm in arm with women in flowing gowns of muslin greeted her eye. A longing sigh escaped her lips as she saw a gentleman help his lady down from a carriage, pressing a gallant kiss on her hand. Absently Ray touched her own wrist as the steady flow of carriages and people on the street mesmerized her senses. It only took her a moment to realize that her own fitted jeans and t-shirt had

76

been replaced by a similar, cream evening gown with a green ribbon tied delicately at the waist. Her hands, encased in matching elegant gloves the colour of clotted cream, almost dropped the book she was carrying as Ray realized that the only thing that remained untouched was her nametag which looked completely out of place on her chest.

"May I?" Before Ray could articulate a response, a pair of white, gloved hands gently unpinned the tag from her dress and placed it in the pocket of an evening jacket.

Her eyes traveled from the gloves wordlessly to James, who too had undergone a transformation. Standing before her in a black coat with shining gold buttons and dark grey breeches, was James smiling crookedly at her. Ray could hardly catch her breath as her heart ached with recognition; James looked like how Ray had always imagined Mr. Darcy, beyond the pages of a character in a novel to the flesh and blood human that existed in the deep recesses of her fantasies.

It was unbelievable what a wardrobe change could do for a person. Never would she mock the 'what not to wear' programs on television again. James looked as though he fit right in with the times, carriages and turn of the century. She noticed absently that the shade of his eyes was the exact color of her ribbon, realizing too late that he had caught her staring shamelessly at him, her eyes shimmering with admiration.

He held out his arm, "My lady."

It felt like a dream, too enchanting to be real, and yet somehow this handsome man in front of her was offering his arm ready to whisk her into a world where she only dared hoped that Jane Austen lived and breathed. Ray lowered her eyes shyly and put her silk gloved hand through his. "You know, I never went to my prom," she said, her voice brimming with emotion as she thought of her mother's crumpled face when she announced that no thank you, she didn't want to go dress shopping for a tradition that had little to do with graduating and more to do with getting smashed. It hadn't even occurred to her that perhaps prom meant something to Eleanor as well; it was a rite of passage she wished her daughter to pass through. But Ray had adamantly refused not knowing that Eleanor had planned a special weekend of prom dress shopping, manicures and bonding for them. She swallowed painfully, "I wish my mother could see this," she whispered.

"You'll be able to tell her all about," he promised.

She nodded, willing back the tears that pooled in the

corner of her eyes.

"Look at your book," he whispered in her ear as they meandered their way through the traffic of carriages and people to the burning lights of the estate to which everyone was making their way towards.

Ray looked down and gasped as the cover of her book had once again magically transformed. She traced her finger lovingly over the gold lettering of 'Pride and Prejudice'.

Oh, Mr. Darcy. A soft sigh escaped her lips. What she had learned of love had begun when she was a child lost in the pages of this book. The manners, the courtesy, the passion, the wit and irony and the best part of all, a single look conveying love and undying devotion. All with cravats properly tied and gowns firmly laced.

It was done with words. Only words. People made love with words and to read about it was as passionate as living and breathing it. And now she was. It was almost too unbearable.

"Would you like a moment alone?" James joked, his voice close to her hair jolted Ray back into reality.

"No thank you, Mr. Darcy and I are quite intimately acquainted," she said with an airy smile, tucking the book back under her arm. "Where are we?" She paused, "James," her eyes grew large, "*When* are we?"

He nodded politely at a passing gentleman with a large monocle as they continued to walk alongside the growing crowd, "The year is 1801. The city, Hampshire. Our pilgrimage tonight, Hampshire Hall, where I hear a Miss Jane Austen is to be attending a ball."

Ray hadn't realized she was digging her nails into the muscles of his arm until he gently pried her fingers loose.

"What's wrong? Would you have preferred the fictitious estate of Pemberley?"

Dates, times and life events were in a chaotic tangle in Ray's mind as she tried to chronologically piece together Jane Austen's life. "Which means that she hasn't moved to Bath yet? And Tom? Tom Lefroy?" Her heart banged against her chest and her mouth became suddenly dry, "James, is Tom here?"

"Lefroy?" his eyebrows drew in concentration, "I believe this is after their unfortunate liaison."

Tom Lefroy and Jane Austen's romance was too dictated by the social whims of society to blossom into marriage. Jane was suffering in the throes of unrequited love, a theme her novels examined but always transcended into marriage. Perhaps art did not always imitate life, Ray thought sadly.

"James, how is any of this real, how could any of this be possible?" her voice came out a whisper as her mind tried to logically assess that she was indeed walking, talking, breathing, and wearing an enchanting gown that she had only seen in film adaptations of Pride and Prejudice, never in real life, never draped on her own body as though they were meant to be there. Sparks of anticipation and thrills of apprehension ran up and down her spine, with bated breath she could only imagine the promises tonight held.

"It feels like a dream," she turned to him with large, earnest eyes, "Please tell me this is real, that I'm awake, that we're really here."

James pressed his lips to her hair and entwined her fingers in his own, "Play pretend. For tonight, it's real."

Ray's heart skipped a beat. It was real. Logically absurd and realistically impossible, but for right now, it was real and she was ready to play the princess of pretend if it meant catching a glimpse or even breathing the same air as Jane Austen. "When does the ball start?" she asked, craning her neck to see past the crowd to their destination. Faint music and echoing laughter could be heard and her skin was electric with excitement. It truly was a feast for her senses.

"There's just one thing, Franchesca," James said, stopping abruptly mid-step.

His voice had turned three shades too serious for Ray's liking and she looked up at him with apprehension. He was going to tell her this was all a dream that she would turn into a pumpkin at the stroke of midnight, that Jane Austen really wasn't here, that...

"Under no circumstances are you allowed to interact with her."

Ray's heart fell. It wasn't as though she was going to rush up to her and give Jane Austen a hug, well, she had thought about it, but social circumstance and propriety wouldn't allow it. That and Jane would think her penchant for physical affection was a bit disconcerting.

"Why?" she ventured to ask in a small voice.

"Because it could potentially affect the future outcome, even a slight alteration could jeopardize everything." He looked at her crestfallen face, "Don't look so sad," he said tipping her chin up with one finger, "The night awaits," he finished with a grand sweep of his arm. Before them the majestic double doors of Hampshire Hall beckoned invitingly, where large chandeliers twinkled brightly overhead bathing the guests in a golden hue. They strolled into the estate with an air of belonging, James smiled and nodded at everyone as Ray drank it all in. Her senses were excruciatingly heightened as she silently vowed to memorize every laugh, every whisper, and every word in the room. And, she thought looking at James, every beat of her heart when his eyes looked back at her.

"For your nerves," he whispered, handing her a champagne flute from a long white table.

Ray held the glass with trembling fingers and downed the contents in one bubbly gulp, took a quick look around to see if anyone noticed and then delicately patted her chin with a napkin. 'Not very ladylike darling', she could hear her mother's voice in her ear. "Am I so obviously nervous?" she asked timidly looking at the elegant dancing couples, illuminated by candlelight.

"No, but you are naturally an alcoholic," James teased, replacing her glass with another, "Drink this one. Slowly," he instructed. He paused, casually observing her over the rim of his glass, "And don't allow anyone to dance with you."

"But they're all so dashing," she said with a laugh, gesturing towards a rotund Colonel flirting with a frightened young girl.

James groaned, "Think ice queen, Franchesca."

Unbidden, a picture of her mother's face floated in Ray's mind. Her mother's reserve, her chilly demeanor when she visited Ray. But Eleanor's expression melted from anger to desperation as Ray recalled her plea to spend Christmas together as a family. *I can't think about that now*, she reprimanded herself sternly. *I'll think about it later, right now I'm in Hampshire.*

Ray forced herself to sip slowly this time as she scanned the room with what she hoped was cool reserve, "Very well, but I don't see why I can't ... Oh, James!" There in the heart of the room came the spirited laughter of a handsome woman.

Her dark hair was pinned up with a becoming arrangement of flowers, her skin was bright with color complimenting her yellow muslin dress similar to the one Ray herself wore. She was chatting animatedly with another lady beside her. Ray could have recognized those unmistakable features anywhere, it was Jane. Jane Austen alive and breathing and giggling barely six feet away from her.

84

Her wide brown eyes met Ray's for a brief moment and she smiled before indulging in conversation with the woman who Ray recognized as her sister, Cassandra.

Her breath caught, "She's beautiful."

James took a sip of red wine, "She is tolerable I suppose, but not handsome enough to tempt me," he quoted with a wink.

"Oh hush, Mr. Darcy," she whispered, her eyes never leaving Jane.

Living, breathing, alive, Jane Austen was but a hop, skip and a jump away and Ray couldn't even thank her for creating one of the greatest literary couples of all time. Dimly she was aware of James commenting upon the moonlight; she nodded politely and continued to watch the scene unfold before her, not daring to avert her eyes even for a moment lest somehow this magical apparition vanished.

Ray's hand remained suspended in the air, as her champagne continued to bubble long forgotten. Jane leaned over to Cassandra who nodded and withdrew to the parlor as Jane quickly gathered her skirts, looked about her once more and made her way discreetly to the rear entrance of the house.

"Where do you think she's going?" Ray asked, her eyes

fixated on the lone figure stealthily sweeping out of the doors. "James?" She patted the space beside her arm distractedly, "James?"

Her hand touched empty air as she realized that James had mentioned something about smokes and cards in the den. Ray doubted he would approve of her following Jane, he would insist that she regain some sense of lost control and not interfere with events. *But,* she thought with a sly smile looking about her, *he wasn't here.*

She picked up the sides of her dress prepared to make an inconspicuous dash towards Jane, when a portly figure obscured her view.

"Well, hello my dear, I don't believe we've had the pleasure of being acquainted," came the jovial voice of a large man. He was dressed in a navy officer's uniform, his stomach protruding, stretching the material to the seams.

"Oh," Ray curtsied in what she hoped was an acceptable manner. The last time she had practiced a curtsey was when she played Ophelia for extra credit in her fourth year Shakespearean seminar.

"Colonel Fitzgerald, at your service, milady," he said with a gallant bow. His hazel eyes turned curiously to Ray, "I don't believe I've seen you before."

"Ah yes, we just got in from Bath, you know, for the season," Ray trilled with a laugh. Lord, she sounded like a bad rendition of Mrs. Bennett.

"I would be most gratified if you would give me the honor of the next dance," he twirled his moustache with his right hand as his eyes appraised Ray greedily.

She lowered her eyes furiously thinking of an excuse to get out of this somehow. Not just to find Jane but also to save herself from the possible molestation from a man at least thrice her age and size. She shuddered at the thought of his beefy arms around her.

"Cold, m'dear?" he asked, prepared to envelop Ray in his heavy coat.

"Fine thanks," Ray said quickly, fixing a bright smile on her face. Her eyes desperately scanned the crowded ballroom for James. "I was just on my way out for some fresh air."

"Nonsense! A bit of dancing will warm you up," he announced with a boisterous nod of his large head. He squinted carefully at her, "You do look a bit pale, let's get some color in your cheeks, then!" He held out his hand to Ray.

"Well that is exceedingly gracious of you Colonel, but -"

"But I believe the next dance is taken," came a deep, familiar voice from over Ray's shoulder. James smoothly intercepted between Ray and her potential dance partner, "Perhaps the next one, Colonel."

"Well I never," he tutted as James whisked Ray to the dance floor.

"I leave you alone for one moment and you catch the eye of the most eligible bachelor in the room," he said with a smile.

"Oh yes, I believe he was the muse for all of Austen's leading men," Ray laughed as he swept her around in an elegant circle. The feel of his arms around her and the soft flickering of candlelight and music almost made Ray forget about Jane's sudden disappearance. He dipped her into a low arch, his lips pressing briefly against the left side of her collarbone, as he whispered in her ear, "Scandalous?"

"Very," she whispered, as he brought her back to him with a slow swoop. Her hands reached up to the nape of his neck, her fingers lost in his brown, tousled hair. She closed her eyes and breathed in the scent of him. It would be so easy to forget why she was here. To just stay in this moment.

Maybe that's what he was doing. Distracting her so she

wouldn't tamper with time and have a conversation with Jane.

A pair of worried eyes searched her own. "Are you alright?" James asked, noting the cloud that had passed over her face.

Ray raised a hand to her temple, a gesture she had seen in countless black and white movies but not one she thought she would be emulating. "Actually, I think I might need some fresh air," she said, her eyes traveling in the direction of the open doors. It wasn't a complete lie either. The way James was looking at her was making her feel more than a little hot under the bonnet. And fresh air would definitely do her some good. Maybe if she hurried she would be able to catch a trace of Jane, wherever she went. Out of the corner of her eye she could see Cassandra's puzzled face as she inquired guests about her sister's whereabouts. "I'll be right back."

"If you must," he bowed, "Hurry back, the dance floor awaits."

"It awaits my two left feet," Ray replied with a quick curtsy. Her heart fluttered as James looked back up into her eyes and for a split second she realized how much she wanted to stay enveloped in the warmth of his arms. Much to her surprise, she blew him a kiss and quickly made her way past the crowded foyer full of gossiping matrons and squealing children and slipped out into the night.

To the left were the gardens and the street from which they had come directly before her to her right. Guided by the soft light of lamps, Ray made her way to the gardens where she hoped Jane was. The cool breeze prickled her skin and she shivered. Once more the feel of James's warm embrace flooded her mind and she felt her cheeks burn crimson with memory. *Jane.* She had to focus on finding Jane. Maybe she would even get to talk to her, she almost squeaked in nervous anticipation at the thought of conversing with Jane Austen. If only she could find her somehow in this maze of bushes.

The garden was a labyrinth of thick rose bushes and apple trees; the rich combination of both intoxicated Ray and she felt, once more, a deep appreciation for the natural world that she had neglected to enjoy.

Stop and smell the roses, her mother had always reminded her. She in turn had rolled her eyes, ignoring the look of hurt that had crossed her mother's face at the time. A pang of guilt washed over her, maybe she ought to start listening to her mother and stop being such a cow. She made a mental note to do so, as she gently plucked a fallen rose from the ground and realizing that she didn't have a pocket, she smiled and tucked it behind her ear.

Hmm, still no sign of Jane. *Where could she be?* Standing up on her tiptoes, Ray strained to see over the tall hedges that obscured her view. It didn't help she was wearing flats.

The sound of a muffled sob met her ears and Ray clapped a hand over her mouth from gasping. *Was that Jane? Was someone hurting her?* Yanking her dainty slippers off her feet and grasping them in her left hand, Ray ran towards the direction of the steadily growing sound of tears. The blood pounded in her veins as her feet flew over the soft ground.

The weeping ceased as Ray turned around a corner. She peeked out into the clearing and saw the silhouette of a familiar figure sitting down, her back shuddering with suppressed sobs. Ray bit her lip, *how could she not help her*? She walked cautiously towards the weeping woman and slipped her shoes back on again, lest Jane think she was an ill-mannered heathen.

"Are you alright?" Instantly she wanted to take back her question, of course she wasn't alright, she was weeping like her whole world was coming to an end.

Jane turned around, "Who's there?" she called out, her

dark eyes alight with fear.

"Just Ray," Ray said with a soft smile. She stepped into the pool of light beside the bench.

"Jane," she replied, hastily wiping her eyes with the back of her hand. "How do you do?"

"Fine thanks. How are you?"

Jane smiled ruefully, her lip trembling, "I'm well, thank you."

"You're a writer Jane, not an actress," Ray teased.

"How do you know about my writing?" she asked, her puffy brown eyes widening in shock.

"Oh, well you know how your father loves to talk about your achievements," Ray said with a light laugh. She strained to summon the information on George Austen's biography and his immense interest and encouragement of his daughter's writing.

"Yes, Father does like to talk," she said with a wan smile.

"He has much to be proud of," Ray said softly. She was struggling to recall if this was before or after Lefroy's engagement to another. Judging by Jane's behavior tonight, she wasn't sure. Just a moment ago she had been laughing without a care in the world with her sister, and now...

Ray bit her lip "Are you alright, Jane?" she asked tentatively. Granted they had just met and Jane had every right to tell her to bugger off and she didn't expect a reply. James would be furious that she had so blatantly disobeyed his instructions and defied him completely, left him alone at the mercy of the ton on the dance floor. She shrugged his inevitable anger away; she couldn't just leave Jane on her own. He would simply have to understand.

"I'm just so overwhelmed," she began softly. With an elegant wave of her hand, she gestured for Ray to join her on the bench, and continued, "I'm tired of it all. I'm tired of not knowing. And all I can do is write it all out so it cannot suffocate me anymore."

Ray nodded sympathetically; she knew all too well what she meant. "Sometimes it's easier that way."

"Precisely," Jane sighed. "It is much easier and there's so much more one can say without the barriers of social propriety dictating every remark uttered from one's mouth."

"At least you *can* write," Ray said jealously looking at the woman who embodied all her inspiration. "You have the power to turn words into stories, sentences into quotes that live on forever, characters that breathe life and love." She looked down at her own hands; hands incapable of creating anything substantial beyond broken chapters and turkey sandwiches. *What was she doing here talking to Jane Austen?* Ray was so inferior in every way possible.

She felt the soft touch of a hand on her shoulder and looked up at Jane, "If you believe so strongly in my ability, how you can doubt your own?"

"Because, Jane, you're magnificent. You're truly an inspiration." Ray knew she shouldn't be saying half these things but she couldn't seem to help herself. "Writing is all I know, but it doesn't mean I do it well or can at all. But *you,* you see things so intricately and can express them so beautifully." Ray turned to her, "You have a gift, Jane."

Jane sat in pensive thought for a moment then exhaled slowly. She raised an embroidered handkerchief to her eyes and then crumpled it into a ball in her hand.

"It's alright," Ray said gently putting an arm around Jane's shoulders. They were so frail; she could feel the outline of each bone. This must have been just after Lefroy's departure and engagement to a woman of more accommodating means. She knew Jane would never marry and would begin to slip into a melancholic depression that would manifest itself in the written word in her more serious, later works; Mansfield Park, Emma and Persuasion. Ray bit her lip wishing there was something she could do or say to the extraordinary woman sitting beside her who was suffering from the world's most common affliction; a broken heart.

"Sometimes the only escape I have is my writing but even then I seem to draw on the realities of a world I am merely a spectator of," Jane sighed, dabbing at her eyes once more.

"But you see things in a way no one else really does. You write about them in such a way that people actually take notice of what's going on and pay attention and examine a shade of truth they were too closed minded to notice in the first place."

Jane turned and looked at Ray with eyes bright with tears, "And what of love? Are all my lovers condemned to the page as well?"

Ray reached over and held Jane's hand tightly, "Your heroes are for eternity. More than any mortal man of flesh and blood, the ones you have created are immortalized in your words," she said her voice thick with emotion. Jane would be a spinster until the day she died and yet her novels, brimming with romance would be classics for the ages. But Jane herself would never know what it felt like to fall asleep in a man's arms, to take sacred vows, to have a family with the man she loved and grow old together.

"Perhaps men in books are better than men in life," Jane said with a little laugh.

"Definitely," Ray nodded in assertion. She lived by that motto. *Perhaps most women did*, she mused. No wonder romances were the most popular genre, every woman did get her prince charming, her happy ending, her true love's kiss and then story was over and the real world was to be reckoned with. "How does one reconcile the two worlds?" Ray mused aloud. But then there was James. She had barely known him barely six hours but she could tell there was something different about him, something rare. Ray paused, "Maybe some people can prove you wrong and you can believe in happily ever afters once more."

"I don't know," Jane responded. She placed her right hand on top of Ray's, "Perhaps it is best not to dwell on what was or what may have been, but dream of what may be."

Ray smiled and squeezed her hand in return, "Beautifully said."

They sat in companionable silence, each woman lost in

her own thoughts when a rush of footsteps broke through their reverie as James and Cassandra turned the corner of the manicured hedge. Cassandra's face was red with exertion and James' darkened with barely suppressed anger.

"There you are!" they both exclaimed in unison.

"We just went out for some fresh air," Ray said defensively, noting the look of controlled fury on James' face. "No harm done," she finished brightly.

"Jane, are you alright?" Cassandra asked noting her sister's red rimmed eyes and pale cheeks.

"Quite fine," Jane assured Cassandra, "We just came out for a turn of fresh air," she inhaled deeply, "Refreshing."

"Very," Ray nodded, hoping that James would stop regarding her with black suspicion.

"Cass, I'd like you to meet Ray," Jane said affectionately holding the crook of Ray's arm.

Ray's heart skipped a beat as she struggled to maintain perfect cordial politeness, "How do you do?" she bowed her head politely.

"It is lovely to meet you," Cassandra said. "I'm so sorry to intrude on your conversation with my sister but Mother would like a word, Jane." She rolled her eyes and whispered conspiratorially to Ray and James, "It's her nerves again."

Ray laughed, it was clear where the inspiration for the unforgettable Mrs. Bennett had come from.

Jane shook her head with an exasperated smile, "Mother and her nerves," she said fondly, "One can't live without the other." She turned politely to Ray, "It was a pleasure meeting you, Ray. I hope we can talk more soon, under happier circumstances."

Ray knew she should have curtsied, maybe bowed a little, shook hands even, but she couldn't help herself from giving Jane a massive hug, squeezing her tightly. Jane Austen was real. A real flesh and blood person and not just a portrait on a poster in her bedroom. "Thank you, for everything," she whispered.

Cassandra looked amused by Ray's outburst of emotion "Are you an American? I did detect a hint of an accent earlier."

"Half," James nodded in assertion, eyeing Ray hard. "Her mother's side."

"Fully English," Ray scowled at him before turning back to Jane, "Tend to your mother Jane, I hope to see you again."

"And I you, Ray," Jane said once more, then in a rush of silk and footsteps, she was gone, leaving only her tears on a handkerchief and the imprint of her fingertips on Ray's own as a testament to her existence. To have conversed with Jane and tasted the thoughts of her mind if only for a brief moment of time was something Ray would treasure for always. Her legs were shaking and she sat down dreamily on the bench once more, her eyes glazed dark silver as she turned to James, "It was Jane. Jane Austen. She liked me." Her voice brimmed with happiness, "She hugged me!"

"I saw," he commented wryly, loosening his cravat. "Believe me, I saw."

Uh oh. "James, I'm sorry, I know I shouldn't have talked to her let alone made physical contact, but I couldn't not! She was crying. And she looked so sad and alone." Her apology flew out of her mouth in a tumble of words as she looked imploringly at him. "It's not my fault I can't control my *American* instincts," she finished pitifully, her lips twitching with laughter.

James didn't say anything.

"Are you mad at me?" Ray whispered, not knowing whether to move closer to him or to edge away. It was hard to read his expression in the moonlit shadows as his prolonged silence grew. "James?"she whispered, placing her gloved hand in his own. "I'm sorry. Did I mess up the future? Are iPods going to take over the world?"

"No."

"Well, that's a good start," Ray said smiling earnestly. "Can you please be nice to me again?"

James brought both of Ray's hands in his own and slowly peeled off each of her gloves. Ray's breath caught in anticipation and she watched with large, liquid eyes as he removed his own gloves and wrapped his arms around her small body, silencing her with his touch. "I'll be nice to you."

Ray peeked up at him through the folds of his cravat, "Promise?"

He sighed in exasperated amusement, "Promise."

"Good," Ray smiled wickedly, jauntily placing his hat upon her head. "Because I wouldn't change a thing."

Chapter V
The Love Child of Paper and Ink

"James, you can't be serious," Ray protested, peering out from under the thick woolen cap he had placed on her head.

"Keep it on, bookworm," he said over his shoulder, "It's going to be a cold one." His own tousled hair was covered in a deep blue hat, a matching scarf wrapped tightly around his neck.

"Well at least you got the color right," Ray muttered. The bright color was the exact shade of crimson Ray adored. The same color she had seen last on her mother's fingernails, she thought with a pang of remorse.

James affectionately patted her hat down over her hair, "It's quite cute, actually. Are you all bundled up?"

Ray held out her arms, "I feel like a marshmallow," she mumbled into her scarf.

Unfazed by the weight of the three layers of clothing in which she was wrapped, James impulsively picked her up and hugged her. "Cushiony," he smiled as he set her back down on the thick snow.

It would take some getting used to, Ray thought trudging

up the snow mountain next to James, his random bursts of affection continued to catch Ray off guard. He either adored her or he wanted to ditch her in the Jurassic period, she couldn't make up her mind which. However at this point it was quite clear that no matter how he felt about her, one thing was for sure, that he was punishing her. Ray placed her hands on her hips and stopped walking again, "Is this my penance, James? Am I so hateful that you must make me climb Kilimanjaro?"

"No. I could think of better ways of inflicting discipline upon you," he said with a throaty chuckle.

Ray's cheeks colored at the double entendre of his meaning. She cleared her throat, "Then why on earth are we mucking about in the snow when I can practically hear a storm brewing!"

"Must you always verge on the dramatic?" he rolled his eyes and held out his hands palms up towards the sky. "There's no storm."

"Oh yeah, the weather is simply *gorgeous*," she said, sarcasm dripping off every word. "Makes me feel like I can conquer the world."

"Oh really? Is that why you go scampering about in

gardens talking to people you mustn't because the weather is simply gorgeous?" he mimicked raising his eyebrow. "Well?"

"I'm much too old to be treated so impertinently," Ray protested crossly folding her arms across her chest, "Jane was upset. I couldn't just leave her there."

He continued walking as though he hadn't heard her and she continued to glare at his retreating back as she grudgingly followed. *Where were they anyway?* They had been walking for hours. Ever since they had left Hampshire Hall, James had somehow managed to lead them on horseback beyond the city, beyond the country side and before Ray could say Yorkshire pudding their clothing had magically transformed to suit their environment. The horse unfortunately had not transformed into a snowmobile, and now here they were mucking about in the snow like they had someplace to be. *Humph.* Ray's eyes narrowed, she wasn't sure what his motives were exactly, he seemed to be taking the mickey out of her, either way, she missed conversing with him. They seemed to be hovering on extremes; arguing or the other thing they did, Ray thought. It wasn't flirting, it felt like something more meaningful, the way the light caught his eyes when he looked at her. Her heart had never skipped so many beats in one day

103

and she had a feeling it was long from over.

The sky was almost white with bright sunlight reflecting on the ground. The snow seemed translucent as though they were walking on diamond clouds. Ray sighed, it really was quite romantic, her dark eyes softened into shades of grey as she looked over at James. Her feet skipped lightly over the snow and she put her thick mitten hand in his. "Hi!"

James looked down at her mitten and then back up at her with a wry smile, "Why am I not surprised?"

"I always come round, James," she said pertly, "And I suppose I've become rather fond of your company, I mean," she looked sideways at him, "It's not like you let me dance with anyone else," she finished cheekily.

He growled in response, but didn't let go of her hand as they kept walking. She stopped suddenly, "James, where's my book?" she patted her coat pockets anxiously, "I don't have it, do you?"

Calmly he unzipped the inside of his jacket, a flash of blue velvet could be seen in his wide inner pockets, "It's safe."

"Good," Ray exhaled, "I was growing rather fond of it," she smiled and then looked about her, "James, not to be a bother but *when* are we exactly?" They had been walking for what seemed like forever to her, though it had most likely been ten minutes and she was starting to get hungry. All the excitement from the ball the previous night had made her too excited to eat and now her stomach was making the most intense growling noises and she thought James was only being too polite of a gentleman to ask her why her stomach could talk.

"Guess."

"Antarctica, the year 400 B.C.?"

"Close."

"Really?"

"No, Franchesca."

"Well at least give me a hint! We could be anywhere in time, James, it's kind of hard to pick and choose a date," she snapped. He was all well and good knowing everything but she felt lost and out of place. She exhaled watching his confident strides out of the corner of her eye. Well at least one of them knew what was going on.

He leaned down next to her ear, and lifted her hat for a second, "It's the Year Without a Summer," James confided with a grin.

Ray gasped. 1816. The Year Without A Summer, the year

scientists claim, eighteen hundred souls froze to death, the year the world was shut away in hiatus due to a volcanic winter resulting from Mount Tambora's eruption the year before. *The Year Without A Summer*. Ray furrowed her eyebrows thinking furiously, the significance of that year tugged at her mind, there had to be a reason it was important.

"Are we going to tour half of Europe, then?" she asked.

"Perhaps just Switzerland," he hinted waiting for his words to sink in.

The Year Without A Summer. *Of course!* It was the year when eighteen year old Mary Shelley created the first science fiction novel. "Frankenstein!" Ray squealed in delight.

"Well the Creature is the hero of the story, after all. Not so much Doctor Frank," James said smiling at her delighted reaction. "I take it you're a fan?"

"James, I love that book! Like, really and truly love it! That book has everything; romance, horror, adventure and the most wonderful protagonist ever written," she sighed.

He gasped in mock horror, "Even more wonderful than your Mr. Darcy?"

"Wonderful in a different way," Ray said with a dreamy smile. "I wish she had named him," she added as an afterthought.

"Victor should have named him," James pointed out.

"He was too frightened," Ray said sadly. Wasn't it just a
moment ago she was in her shop, holding the frayed copy to
her chest. Her heart constricted as she recalled the whole
story of how the dejected, banished Creature having no refuge
after he was turned out by his creator, Victor Frankenstein,
suffered at the hands of mankind immensely. She felt chills
run down her spine as she realized that James had brought
her to the very Swiss Alps that had inspired Mary Shelley to
craft her haunting tale. She felt a bit like the poor Creature
now, lost and confused, and more than a little peckish.

A cold drop of rain fell on the tip of her nose as the sky
began to darken ominously with thunder clouds. It all
happened so suddenly Ray didn't have time to ask whether
they were close to their destination, or what their destination
even was at this point. She could see no trace of human life,
nor shelter, just a vast expanse of nothing. The sky cracked
open and the rain began to fall faster and faster around them.

"Hurry!" Using his coat to shelter them both from the
ruthless lashing of cold rain drops, James and Ray began
running. She had no idea where they were going, her eyes

were squeezed shut and her only instinct was to blindly follow him wherever he was taking them. It was then Ray realized with a sudden lurch of her stomach that had nothing to do with hunger, that she trusted this person she met barely twenty four hours ago with her life.

"Just a little bit further!" he shouted encouragingly, mistaking her slowing pace for fatigue rather than the weight of the epiphany she had just had. "Just a little bit more. I see smoke, there must be a house nearby."

She nodded and ran alongside him, clasping his hand tighter as the rain continued to fall down around them like a relentless waterfall. Though James had raised his coat around them like a cape, her vision was still blurry and her feet stumbled on the slick, slippery snow. Her legs felt sluggish and immovable as though she had been caught in Medusa's stony stare. She pushed her wet bangs out of her eyes and for a moment she could see a tall chimney puffing thick clouds of smoke despite the torrential weather. Her foot stumbled on a snow bank and her body lurched forward, her face was only inches from striking the ground when a strong pair of arms whisked her up into a warm haven of fabric.

Through the blur of rain and wind, Ray looked up at

James; his jaw was taught, his teeth gritted and his hair pressed against his face made him look paler with exertion.

"James, I can walk, it's alright," she protested.

His eyes met hers briefly and he smiled, shaking his head, "We're halfway there."

Halfway? There was more to go. She groaned inwardly but pressing her cheek against the warm comfort of his jacket, she realized she didn't mind.

They were living on a prayer and her faith in his stamina, Ray thought wearily, turning her neck to look out at the shadowy silhouette of the large manor that was slowly becoming clearer. She tucked her head back under his chin, his light 5 o'clock shadowy beard tickling her slightly and said a silent prayer that someone would be home to let them in.

They finally arrived at the majestic gates of the estate. It looked like something out of a Gothic novel she had read, like a cross between Vlad the Impaler's fortress and a fairy tale castle. High, iron spires reaching to the skies creaked ominously as James pried the gates open. Ray shivered, her mind flooded with flashback scenes from horror movies, "James, what if this is a bad idea?" she yelled over the sounds of impeding rain. The sky flashed with a bolt of lightning followed by an earth shattering crack of thunder.

"What's the alternative?" he shouted grimly, setting her down. "Are you alright?" his eyes flashed concern as she wobbled unsteadily.

"I'm fine," she assured him, even through her heart was racing and every inch of her was drenched in cold, freezing water. She leaned up on tiptoes and pushed his thick wet hair back, "Are *you* alright?" He looked paler than usual, his lips an odd shade of blue, "James?"

He clenched his jaw, gritting his teeth to keep them from chattering with the cold, "I'm fine, Franchesca."

"You're not. You're blue!"

"It's the new tan."

"James, really, are you feeling alright?" Her eyes searching his face for signs of sickness or fatigue.

"Just peachy," he smiled, pressing a wet kiss on her forehead. He held her hand and with his other arm and used his jacket like a protective cloak around them once more. "We should be fine," he assured her, "I hear Lord Byron is quite an affable host."

Ray's heart stopped as she turned to look at James incredulously. "What did you just say?" rainwater sputtering from her open mouth.

"What?" Another crack of thunder followed and James gestured for her to start running again. "Hurry!" The rain slapped against their skin painfully as they hurried over the cobbled entrance towards the large oak doors of the magnificent chateau. Ray recognized it immediately as Villa Diodati, Byron's rented vacation home.

Which meant that not only were they in Switzerland, in the Year Without A Summer, but in the midst of a gloomy, incessant rain storm. Her heart thudded against her chest as she turned to James with luminous eyes, "James, is Mary Godwin in there writing Frankenstein?"

"Not Godwin," he corrected as they ducked underneath the high archway leading to the entrance, "Shelley. She eloped two years ago." He raised his fist to the door, then paused, turning to Ray, "And maybe."

With a flourish the door opened and standing before them in a billowing dressing gown stood one of the great Romantic poets, Lord Byron himself. His floppy dark hair whirled in the torrential storm as he ushered them inside. "Come in! Come in! Surely it is the weekend of lovers and bad weather! Come in!"

With quick steps he led them to the large den where a toasty fire was crackling, "Mary! Claire! Fetch warm clothes and towels for our new friends," he patted Ray's hand sympathetically, "You look as though you've seen a ghost, my dear. Come, let me seat you by the fire," he said kindly, leading Ray towards a cozy ottoman.

Ray couldn't take her eyes off him. There he was, Lord Byron. Of course she looked like she had seen a ghost, he had been dead for nearly two hundred years, and yet, she looked helplessly at James to make sense of this madness, and yet, he was here in flesh and blood, just like Jane Austen had been, talking to her, asking Mary Shelley to fetch her clothes. She felt her head start to swim, it was much too much to take in.

"Careful!" Byron lurched forwards, pushing himself between James and Ray. He caught her fully by the waist, laying her down on the sofa.

"James?" Ray murmured weakly, her eyes closed with fatigue.

"Byron, actually," he said, gracefully pulling a red afghan off an armchair and gently covered Ray with it. "She needs to change into something warm and eat," he murmured half to himself. Pressing the palm of his hand on Ray's forehead he turned to James, "She might have a fever."

"No, I'm fine really," she insisted, raising her head. Her eyes kept closing of their own accord as she struggled to keep them open, she wanted to drink in every single detail, every syllable, every word, every influx of each voice echoing around her, to commit this moment to memory, to...

"Rest," James commanded softly, fully aware of Ray's intentions to memorize everything that was occurring. "I'll get you an autograph, if you promise to relax," he whispered, his breath tickling her ear.

His voice was a warm balm that spread from her wet hair down to her freezing toes and Ray almost pulled him down next to her until she realized that he too was dripping with cold rain, just like her. "Come." She opened her arms out and beckoned James to clamber in the warmth of the afghan, "You're freezing too."

"Yes! Body heat!" Byron exclaimed settling himself between Ray and James, "We'll be right as rain in no time," he joked with a jovial laugh.

Ray suppressed a laugh as James scowled at the back of Byron's head. Their host's hefty arms were happily around each of their shoulders pressing them close to his sides. "You

113

came just in time," he said, his eyes bright, "We were just about to tell ghost stories!"

Ray's mouth dropped open, *surely this couldn't be the fateful day, the summer afternoon of Frankenstein?* The night where Mary, inspired by a nightmare crafted the story of Victor Frankenstein's sublime creation. Ray craned her neck over Byron's head to look at James in wonder, he had brought her here on purpose, of that she was sure. Words couldn't describe how much it meant to her.

Green eyes met brown and he smiled at Ray mischievously, "Think you can handle a few scary stories tonight?"

"Only if you promise to stay right here," Ray responded shyly.

Byron finally grasped the situation and he abruptly stood up, "I'll see to Mary and Percy. You really must meet them. Oh, and Claire," he added as an afterthought, his face falling slightly. "Just a moment, dear friends," he said with an elaborate move towards the salon door.

James frowned at his retreating back, "Friendly, that one," he observed darkly.

Ray looked at his face and burst into laughter, "James,

he's bi. It's ok. I'm sure he wanted to sit next to you more than me."

"Really?"

"Yeah, too bad they don't teach you that sort of thing in middle school," she grinned and motioned for him to come closer, "In fact, he kind of has a thing for Percy."

"Percy Shelley?"

She nodded. "I'm pretty sure I read that there was also an instance of incest as well, if I remember correctly. But who really knows."

James grimaced, "Poets are an odd bunch, aren't they?"

Ray, sniffed disdainfully, "James, these aren't just any sidewalk poets, they're the Romantics. Byron, Percy, they're up there with Wordsworth and Keats," she frowned in concentration, "Well not, Byron. He's not technically part of the 'Great Six'," she said in air quotes, "But he's wonderful in his own right and ... WE'RE IN HIS LIVING ROOM!" she finished with a shriek.

James clapped a hand over her mouth, "He'll think you're mental."

She nipped his fingers with her teeth, "Just tell him I'm delirious with fever," she looked at him, eyes shining. "James, first Jane Austen, now this," she placed his hand on her chest, "I don't think my heart can take much more of this."

The doors flung open as a small party of people and trays of tea entered the salon, "Young lovers!" Byron boomed to Percy with a wink as he saw Ray and James' close proximity to one another, "Can't keep their hands off each other."

Ray froze in temporary shock as the group of the most brilliant, most famous writers and poets came towards her in their bedclothes. James squeezed her hand reassuringly, "Breathe," he whispered before they stood up and shook hands with everyone. Mary Shelley was every bit as lovely as her portrait. It was hard to believe she had given birth to her second child a mere five months ago, she looked so frail. Her gentle gray eyes studied Ray inquisitively, "Byron told us you were lost in this storm," she shook her head sympathetically and handed Ray a stack of towels and a cotton nightgown, "I hope this fits, we seem to be the same size, well almost," she said with a laugh as she realized that Ray was about a foot smaller than she was. "Either way, it's quite warm."

Ray smiled gratefully, "The fire warmed us nicely, but a gown would be lovely, thank you." *She couldn't believe it, she was sharing bedclothes with Mary Godwin-Shelley!*

"I believe Percy has a robe that would fit you nicely," Mary said with a smile. "I'll go get it."

"Oh really, don't trouble yourself," James insisted.

But Ray could see his face was still two shades too pale, his hands brittle with cold. She took a towel and ruffled his hair with it, "Would you like my nightgown instead?" she teased.

Mary laughed, "I'll be right back with the robe."

"All taken care of." A voluptuous brunette in an almost transparent blue nightgown entered the room, a silk robe draped over her arm. She walked up to James and handed him the robe. "How do you do? I'm Claire."

"And I'm Ray," Ray said with a bright smile, sticking her hand into Claire Claremont's; Mary Shelley's step-sister and childhood rival. Claire was an interesting personality Ray had come across in many history books. She was known for her very great and not very discreet passionate nature regarding men in general and Byron in particular. Ray suppressed a smile, she was quite sure Claire was with child. Byron's love child. Funny how that didn't stop her from flirting with James, she thought, narrowing her eyes at the woman who was currently enraptured with James' account of the storm.

117

"Oh, Claire," Percy Shelley muttered, rolling his eyes. Like Byron, who was more animated, a larger than life figure whose portrait did shame to his whimsical personality, Percy was just as Ray had imagined him to be; tall, with an unruly mass of light brown hair, his eyes blazing rebel fire.

Ray was momentarily transfixed by the intensity of his gaze, "Pleased to meet you," she stammered.

"A pleasure," Percy replied warmly, shaking both her and James' hand. "Please, make yourselves comfortable, the rain doesn't seem to be letting up anytime soon. The Gods are displeased tonight." Ray noticed his fingers were stained with ink and she wondered what poem he had been penning earlier.

"They've been displeased the whole rotten summer, dear boy," Byron said with a booming laugh as he and Mary began to set the tea tray by the fire.

Before Ray could offer to help, Percy gently took her by the arm and gestured towards a powder room, "I believe you can change there, at your convenience."

Ray nodded, her eyes fixed on Claire.

"Don't worry about her," he whispered with a smile. "Now go change and come before the tea gets cold!" he whistled at

Claire, "Kindly remove yourself from the man and let him change." He ushered James and Ray towards the arched doorway and into a brightly lit hallway. "I believe Ray can show you where the powder room is," Byron said with a sly wink. "Don't be too long," he said gesturing towards a tray laden with steaming tea and thick slices of bread and butter, "I can't promise this will be here when you return. We poets need our nourishment!"

His laughter was infectious and Ray found herself smiling as she and James strolled towards the small room at the end of the large hall, their footsteps muffled by the thick carpet. "I can't believe this!" she whispered excitedly.

"I know."

"I wonder if I could eBay this," she said with a grin, fingering the delicate fabric of the nightgown.

"You could always try," he laughed. "I don't know who would believe you." They had reached the end of the hall where a burning candle on a brass stand flickered precariously.

Ray tentatively took the candle in her hand, "Do you want to go first?"

He bowed deeply, "Ladies first, my love."

Love? Ray felt warm despite her wet clothes, "Actually James, you're frozen, you go first. It's ok, I'll wait," she turned the brass handle with the other and shoved him gently through the door. "Go."

"So demanding," he joked taking the candle from Ray and closing the door behind him.

Ray exhaled and leaned against the polished oak. She couldn't believe any of this. Byron's deep laugh echoed in the hallway and she had to bite her lip from squealing in pure excitement. Claire's shrill voice could be heard too after a moment. Ray felt her lips purse in annoyance, why was she getting upset, it wasn't as though James was her boyfriend. He was her companion, her really lovely, really wonderful, really protective, really gorgeous companion. She swallowed and felt her cheeks burn, as James emerged from the bathroom clad in a deep blue silk robe, a towel slung around his neck, his hair slicked back from his forehead and his eyes burning green flames into her own.

"Fits well," she managed to say, as he moved closer to her.

"It's surprisingly warm," James replied. He pressed a hand to her cheek, "You look kind of warm, are you feeling ..."

"James!" Claire high voice trilled from across the salon,

"Hurry, we're about to start!"

He didn't takes his eyes off Ray. "Franchesca, I..."

"Yes?" Ray said breathlessly. She laced her fingers through his, his face was inching closer to hers, his breath warm against her cheek.

"James!" came Claire's insistent cry. And just like that the spell was broken.

"In a moment." he called out.

"No, actually, go right ahead," Ray said turning away. Her fingers on the door handle.

"What? No."

"James, go. What are you waiting for?" Ray swallowed thickly. She knew she was being unreasonable but he didn't have to wait for her, he didn't have to do anything for her.

"Go. I'll be fine."

"Franchesca..."

"Claire's waiting," she snapped. She saw his hurt and confused face before she closed the door firmly behind her and wished she could take back the last ten seconds of her life. *What was wrong with her*, she thought angrily stripping off her shoes and socks and attacking the buttons on her shirt. Here she was with the greatest poets in society and all she could think of was the way Claire had looked at James.

Well, she could look at him whichever way she wanted, it wasn't as if Claire was married to Byron and it wasn't as though Ray was dating James or anything. She yanked the nightgown down over her head and groaned when she saw the deep pink fabric trail on the floor. It was too long. Well hopefully they wouldn't be looking at her feet.

Dear Lord, she raised her eyes to the mirror above the sink, she looked like she had been shipwrecked. Her eyes were slightly bloodshot, her skin unusually pale, save for her cheeks; bright with excitement and colored with confused shame as she thought of the last expression on James' face.

Ray quickly ran her fingers through her long, dark hair, making a mental note to book an appointment with Paula the moment she was home.

Home.

Would she ever be home again? She chewed her lower lip as she gazed at her reflection, "Do you even want to go back home?" she whispered to the girl staring back at her in the mirror.

A sudden crack of thunder reverberated and Ray could hear the shrieking cries of the women in the salon.

The lights went out. The powder room was consumed with a thick smoky darkness that was suffocating. Her hand reached for the brass handle and pulled frantically. It wouldn't budge. Ray was stuck.

Another crack of thunder resounded followed by lightning that bathed the whole room in light from the window overhead. She caught sight of her pale reflection in the mirror and screamed; it was like seeing a ghost.

Oh God, what if she was in a house surrounded by ghosts. Mary was dead. Byron and Shelley were dust in graves. *She knew they had died, how was this possible, how was this real?* She squeezed her eyes shut furiously trying to erase the thought from her mind. The hairs at the back of her neck rose and she felt her skin crawl with fear.

"Franchesca!"

"James!"

She clawed at the door, grasping at the handle, "I can't open it!"

"You have to stay calm," he said soothingly on the other side, "Just let go of the handle, I'll open it from the outside."

Her eyes still shut, Ray tried to take deep breaths to stop her body from shaking. She could hear James outside and she knew she would be safe.

"Stand back," James wrenched open the door just as Ray jumped back, her back pressed painfully against the marble sink.

"Are you okay?" The brass candle in his hand illuminated the worry etched on every line of his face.

Ray fell into his arms and pressed herself close against him. "I am now."

He pressed his lips against her hair, "Sure?"

She closed her eyes and nodded against his chest waiting for her heart to stop pounding. "Please don't go," she whispered.

"I won't leave you."

"The lights have gone out!" Byron exclaimed jovially, as they returned back to the party gathered by the fireplace, "So we shall have to make do with traditional candlelight and fire," he looked at Ray with concern, "I hope you are alright, we heard a scream and before we could even move, James had rushed to you *quick as lightning*," he chuckled to himself while Percy groaned at his friend's pun. "But truly," Byron continued nodding in approval at James, "I could use a lad like you."

Ray bit back a grin as James nodded and awkwardly

stepped over Claire's unnecessarily exposed legs to the couch where the afghan Lord Byron had bestowed upon Ray earlier, was spread out invitingly. James looked up at Ray, "Coming?"

She curled up on his lap like she had seen Molly curl up in her favourite chair with the tattered pink cushion countless times. She tucked her head under his chin, a cup of tea grasped in her right hand and his hand in her left.

As everyone gathered around the fire with large blankets and soft slippers, James put a piece of hot buttered bread in Ray's mouth every now and then as though he was feeding a bird. Ray bit at his finger playfully and closed her eyes as she leaned against his chest. Everything felt so perfectly surreal right now. Here, in Mary Godwin's nightgown with a cup of tea and a whole afternoon of candlelight and conversation stretched out before her.

"Such a wet, uncongenial summer," Mary said with a sigh. "Even our friend, John Polidori is ill with some sort of flu." She hovered by Shelley's arm and stared gloomily into the fire, "However, today we have guests," she said with a smile, "How would you like to pass the time until the storm lets up?"

Ray looked at James slyly before turning back to Mary, "Perhaps a story?"

Byron clapped his hands enthusiastically and Mary looked at Ray in astonishment, "That is how we've been we have been spending our days together. What a coincidence!"

"I'll say," James muttered under his breath, looking at Ray with a mixture of exasperation and amusement.

"Wonderful!" Byron pointed to a selection of books on a table by the fire place, "So far we've been reading Goethe's *Faust*, Eyries' *Fastasmagoriana*..."

"Oh!" Mary clapped a hand over her mouth, "I have been having the most atrocious nightmares as of late," she turned to Ray, "Truly these stories can make one's imagination run a little wild."

Ray nodded, "I can imagine," she recalled her own sleepless nights induced by Faust's *Mephistopheles* tempting her with devilish delights. She patted Mary's hand reassuringly, "We've all had nights like those where all your worst fears come to life but when you wake up the next morning, you know it's just a dream."

"Nightmare," Mary corrected grimly. "Although," she began slowly, "Since we have exhausted our library, I vouch we tell our own ghost stories this afternoon."

"Let's make it into a grand competition!" Byron added

with a clap of his hands

"What do you think, Ray?" Mary asked with a smile, "Do you like ghost stories?"

"Love them." Ray grinned in eager anticipation, practically bouncing on the sofa. This was it. The night of Frankenstein, or at least the nightmare that inspired the novel. She felt James' arms around her, in an effort to keep her barely suppressed excitement suppressed. Ray snuggled into his arms, there was no one else she would have wanted by her side right now. He pulled the afghan tighter around them and rested his cheek against her hair.

"If you will excuse me," Claire said dramatically standing up, "I am not fond of stories of crude and wild natures," she looked pointedly at Mary, "I'm a lady of taste."

If she wasn't engulfed in layers of fabric and contentedly chewing on buttered bread, Ray would have jumped up to the defence of Mary's preference for stories.

Percy shrugged, "Do as you please. I believe John may still be awake, playing cards in the salon."

"Well then, you automatically lose," Byron shrugged. "Such a shame, Claire."

"Lose what?" Ray asked curiously.

"Lose his little story contest," Claire said contemptuously. Ray bit back a smile as she recalled what she had read about Claire's inability to write as well as the other poets present in the room. She didn't even try anymore and attempted to use her sexuality to gain leverage as an intellect. Ray gave her a polite smile, "What was your story called, Claire?"

"I prefer to listen than to narrate," she said haughtily.

"Well I had narrated 'A Fragment' last night," Bryon said with an apologetic smile at his guests. "Had you been here for that it would have positively made your skin crawl," he said cheerfully, biting into a thick slice of buttered bread.

"Shame," Claire said dismissively. She turned to James, her eyes inviting, "Do you play cards, James?"

"I prefer stories," James replied, smiling at Ray.

"Actually, I have a story," Mary began slowly, her eyes traveling from one person to another. "Well," she paused, "It's more of a waking dream."

Ray felt her breath constrict, this was it! Mary's inspiration for Frankenstein, related in flesh and blood. She squeezed James' hand, she couldn't believe this was actually happening.

Mary brought a candle close to her face, her luminous

eyes glowing, she paused, "This is a true story," she whispered, and with a breath of air, blew the flame out.

"When I placed my head upon my pillow, I did not sleep, nor could I be said to think," her voice lowered, "I saw -- with shut eyes, but acute mental vision--I saw the pale student of unhallowed arts kneeling beside the thing he had put together. I saw the hideous phantasm of a man stretched out, and then, on the working of some powerful engine, show signs of life, and stir with an uneasy, half-vital motion," her hands began to shake. Percy reached over to hold his wife, but Mary dismissed his reassuring touch. She took a deep breath and continued, "Frightful must it be; for supremely frightful would be the effect of any human endeavor to mock the stupendous Creator of the world."

The air was thick with silence when Mary had finished narrating her story, the only sound was the crackling fire. Every shadow on the wall was the creature of Mary's nightmare, Ray thought with a shiver. James pulled her closer, "It's only a story," he whispered softly.

"It will be," she said. Having only read Frankenstein in the light of a classroom, dissecting its themes of unholy creation and Victor's unsuccessful subversion of natural law, Ray was brought back to the true essence and the monstrosity of it all. She shuddered, her eyes traveling to the quiet teenager whose tale would leave an imprint in history for generations to come.

They stayed there all night, feasting on imagination and what seemed to be an endless supply of hot tea, until the first rays of dawn began to spread, seeping through the stained glass windows, bathing everything in coloured light. It was hard to imagine that such a clear, perfect sky had been monstrous half a day ago.

"You simply must stay," Byron implored James as he announced that he and Ray ought to be taking their leave.

"That is exceedingly gracious of you but we really must be going," James said apologetically.

"Must we?" Ray asked sleepily. She rubbed her eyes and looked at James, "Must we?" she repeated with a small pout. She was in literary paradise and James was taking her back to earthly plains.

"We must," James said.

"Then allow me to give you use of my carriage and horseman, Arthur," Byron said generously. "And sadly, we must bid one another adieu," he said taking both of Ray's hands in his own.

Percy shook hands with James and Ray, "If you ever get lost again, find us."

"Mary, your gown," Ray began fumbling with the ribbons at the high neckline, "Just give me a moment and I'll -"

Mary handed Ray her clothes from the night before, "The maid pressed these for you, they should be dry," she smiled at Ray, "I would've told you to keep the gown, but it is awfully big on you," she said with a laugh, watching Ray try not to trip as she went to the powder room to change.

"Well, Mary, you are a good, healthy height," Ray said with a sleepy smile splashing cold water on her face from a jug by the basin. As she folded the pink fabric to give back to her hostess she pressed it up against her face, inhaling it; it was real, last night had been real, this whole thing was real. She giggled to herself as she recalled her horror at being locked in the powder room last night, shaking her head at her reflection, Mary wasn't the only one with an overactive imagination, she thought wryly.

Mary was leaning against the door waiting for Ray, "Must you leave?" she asked forlornly when Ray emerged wearing her snow clothes.

"Sadly," Ray replied, "But you'll be fine," she grinned

mischievously, "You have Claire."

Mary rolled her eyes, "Any further words of encouragement?"

"Keep writing," Ray whispered, squeezing Mary's tiny hand in her own.

"I haven't started," Mary said with a laugh, looking curiously at Ray, "Well I've been thinking about it but I haven't really ...

"You will," Ray promised "And when you do it shall be sublime."

Mary's gray eyes grew wide, "Really?"

"Of course. It's in your blood." Ray said, putting her red wool cap over her head. "Your mother passed on her gift to you and now with it, you can haunt the world with Victor Frankenstein's creation," she smiled at Mary, observing for the second time how truly young she was. She was slightly in awe at how this young girl's imagination would inspire countless books, movies, Halloween costumes and generations of readers.

Mary pulled Ray into a fierce hug, "I've always meant to write, something to get it all out of me, mother's death, my daughter's..." her voice broke, "It's just the extreme balance between what we know as life and what we strive to create, and perhaps, recreate if we could."

"Put pen to paper, Mary, nothing can stop you," Ray said. As with Jane, Ray could scarcely believe what she was doing, who she was embracing, and yet, somewhere in the back of her mind, a voice told her this couldn't possibly be happening, that none of this could be real, but as she stepped out into the sunlight with James by her side and an open carriage awaiting them, she knew that she had begun to believe in a magic she couldn't explain.

Chapter VI
The Lady Doth Protest

The carriage gently rolled along the scenic European countryside as the morning sun shone in through the painted glass windows. A kaleidoscope of colors fell onto Ray's lap as she lazily observed the shimmering hues of blue and gold. Stretching luxuriously in the purple cushion lined coach she could hear the rhythmic sound of hooves and the rustle of wind outside and vaguely wondered where they were. Snuggling closer to the warmth of the arms wrapped around her, she smiled dreamily to herself. Maybe she was still dreaming, this couldn't be real.

"James?" Her voice was soft and muffled with sleep. No response. She tilted her head where it was tucked beneath his chin and looked up to see if he was still sleeping.

His eyes were closed; his dark lashes a striking contrast to his pale skin. His mouth was slightly open as he breathed deeply. Ray gently loosened the scarf around his neck with trembling fingers. She had never been so close to him without him being awake. She hadn't really dared. There was something so precariously wonderful about being near him, as though his mere presence was enough for her whole being.

She bit her lip, he really did look dashing. Even half asleep he was beautiful, innocent and completely hers for the time being. Resisting the urge to run her fingers through his thick wavy hair, she leaned up and looked at him with heavily lidded eyes and gently traced the outline of his mouth with her fingertip. "Wakey," she whispered.

He shook his head sleepily, "No."

"Please, James." Ray leaned up and pressed a kiss on the side of his jaw.

He caught her hand in his. "Franchesca," he murmured. *Thrills.*

He thrilled her. The sound of her name on his lips, the look that had passed between them last night before Claire had interrupted them, he moved her in ways that no boy ever had. Her heart ached a little as she realized that she must be so ordinary to him while he was so heartbreakingly extraordinary to her, like magic.

Speaking of ordinary, what did she even look like?

She caught her reflection in the window opposite and self-consciously patted her dishevelled hair into place and pinched her cheeks for a bit of extra color, just like in the books she used to read about women who lived pre-blush-available-in-thirty-different-shades times.

Were they in those days now? What days were they in?

Sleeping James or not, curiosity got the best of Ray as she threw back the curtains and was temporarily blinded by the light of the sun. No longer could she see houses or even a road. The frosty, winding streets of the Swiss Alps were left behind many miles ago, as their carriage made way through the heart of the country.

To her left James groaned sleepily.

"James?" Ray tapped his cheek gently with her hand.

"Sleeping," he murmured.

"At least tell me where we are?" she insisted. "We're quite far off the mainland."

James cracked open one hazy eye, light green with sleep and looked down at Ray's upturned face. "We should've been there by now," he muttered with a yawn. He turned his neck from left to right and Ray winced when she heard a crack. When he stretched it seemed as though he was taking up all the room in the carriage with his long limbs. He was like a waking giant trapped in a gilded cage.

Ray curled up to the side against the window. "Been

where?"

"How long have we been travelling?" James asked, ignoring her question. He loosened his scarf and fixed her with a questioning green gaze. "Well?"

Ray lifted her hands up in a shrug, "I don't know. I just woke up too." Her stomach growled. "And so did my appetite." She blushed.

"Aye." James pinched Ray's cheek as he leaned across and opened the basket Lord Byron had generously given to them as they left. He pulled out a red apple, "Eat."

Ray took the fruit and took a huge bite, apple juice dripping down her lip. She couldn't recall the last time she had eaten such a crunchy piece of fruit.

"Such a lady."

"Naturally," she munched happily. She held it out to him, "Bite?"

James shook his head, pulling back the curtains and turned the latch on the window as a rush of fresh country air flew into the carriage.

"Eee!"

"Cold?" he quickly closed it half way.

"Don't!" Ray clambered up on the seat next to him and

unceremoniously stuck her head out the window.

"Franchesca!"

She ignored him. The wind whipped through her hair and the sun shone gloriously on her face. She inhaled deeply, her lungs breathing in the sweet essence of pure air. Nothing had felt so wonderful. Except for James pulling on her hand to get her away, she thought wryly, as she sat back dejected on the thick cushioned seat.

"Must you do things like that?"

"I must," she nodded with a bright smile. "James you don't understand, I can't even explain it, I just..." her voice trailed off as she sought to find the right words to express how free she felt, how at peace and at wonder with the world around her, "I just need this," she finished softly.

He settled back into his seat watching her closely, "I understand."

Ray smiled and turned back to the scenery, her eyes following every tree as it flew by her peripheral vision. Her body swayed to and fro as the carriage continued to amble contently on the winding road. "James, where are we going now?"

"Nowhere, in particular," he responded, stretching his

long legs out in front of him in the carriage, "I thought we could just hang out."

Since when did he not have a plan? "Hang out?"

"Hang out."

Ray looked back at him over her shoulder, "Sounds good." She crawled back to her seat beside him and laid her head serenely on his shoulder and closed her eyes. She had never felt so rested as she had been when she was with him, granted that luxury only came about when they were on the brink of fever in Lord Byron's Villa or in the backseat of a moving carriage going God knows where, she still savored every moment she had with him. The thought of it all coming to an end never entered her mind.

"Tell me about your bookshop."

"Hmm?"

He smiled into her hair, "Tell me about the bookshop where you're from."

"Oh," Ray absently fingered her name tag. "It's pretty much my home, I suppose. It's an absolute mess," she said with a laugh, "But I think it's always been a mess, ever since my father used to live there," her voice grew soft. It was always a painful subject talking about her father. She always tried to avoid the conversation altogether, but with a mother like Eleanor who wasn't quite prepared to let sleeping ghosts lie, she found herself thinking about him more and more often. How could she not, she lived in the last place he had been alive.

"What was your father like?" he asked gently.

"Wonderful and intelligent and kind," she exhaled softly, "He felt like home."

"And your mother?"

"My mother is something else entirely," she said with a laugh, thinking of her mother's last visit. Her eyes grew dim as she recalled the words she had said to her, "My mother is... interesting," she finished.

"Do you see your interesting mother often?" he asked.

"Sometimes." She tensed.

"Only sometimes?"

"I'm busy James, I have an actual shop to run, books to order and catalogue and *if* I have time leftover I try to write my book. My book which by the way I have been working on for ages," she said defensively, "I just can't seem to find the time and with the holidays there're all these expectations and stuff..." her voice trailed off as she realized shamefully how

140

weak her own excuses sounded to her ears. "I suppose I just miss how my family used to be," she conceded, recalling with misty eyes how happy her mother and father had once been. Her most treasured memories were of her parents reading stories to her as she lay on the rug by the fireplace. But evenings like that had become few and far between when her father had started to work late and her mother had begun resenting his priorities, or lack of them and their marriage had crumbled. Stony silence would stretch on for days at a time, and there was nothing that Ray could do as a child, or much that she could understand. "It doesn't get better."

James tilted her chin up and gently wiped the stray tear that trickled down her cheek, "I'm sorry."

Hot tears slipped down her face and onto her lap, "Me too."

"It's ok." He traced gentle circles on her back. "It's ok."

It wasn't. But maybe it could be. Ray nodded, tucking her head into the folds of his blue shirt, "Tell me about you."

"What about me?"

"Who are you?"

"I'm a reluctant time traveler," he said with a congeneial smile that gave nothing at all away. "Tell me about yourself."

141

"I'm the bookkeeper's daughter," she paused, "And an accidental time traveler."

"Believe me, this was no accident."

Ray paused and mulled that over. She was meant to fall into this warped abyss and meet James. She was meant to meet these amazing, incredible women who inspired her to write. *But why? What was the overall purpose of this journey? Where would it lead them?* Unbidden, the thought of James taking her to a final destination and leaving her, made her throat dry and her eyes prickle.

She closed her eyes and felt him cradle her cheek with the palm of his warm hand, "What's wrong?"

"Nothing."

"What kind of nothing?" he persisted.

"Can we talk about something else, please?"

"Like what?"

"Tell me a story," she hiccupped.

"What kind of story?"

"Any story, but my own."

"You can always create and recreate your own story," he said, "Just as long as you don't go to the extremes like our friend Victor Frankenstein." James pressed his lips into her hair, "And believe me you're nothing like Victor Frankenstein."

She smiled a little, as he knew she would. "I suppose. I don't know, I think everything was better before, you know, or that nothing can be as good as I imagine it to be," she exhaled, "I don't know, I just really don't know." Her head felt heavy with the burden of her thoughts, how nice it would be to not have to think anymore, to not have to feel anymore. She recalled a picture of a smiling pastry that read, 'Life would be easier if I was a bagel.' It was true.

"You can't do this."

Her voice cut short the ribbon of Ray's thoughts, "Pardon me?"

"Franchesca, no two moments are the same."

Wait, what? She leaned back on her elbow and looked up at him.

James looked at her carefully, his green eyes penetrating her dark ones, and repeated his words slowly, hoping they would register fully, "No two moments are the same."

Ray crossed her arms defensively, "I am painfully aware of that fact, thank you."

"No, you're not. You keep trying to recreate something

extraordinary you had or something that you want desperately in your mind, and you can't. You can't expect things to be as they were and you can't keep reliving memories of ..."

Ray held up her hand, "Please, don't. I'm trying not to think about it." Even without saying his name, she felt the absence of her father's loss once again. Granted, over the years the raging anguish had now dulled to a hollow numbness. She didn't know which was worse. Both hurt. Still. Always.

"How can you not talk about it when it's all you think about?"

"Maybe I don't want to think about it anymore." She scowled at the remaining apple in her hand, "I know I should be thinking about my future, or something along those lines. And there's so much I want to do with my life. I want to write and see the world and not be stuck ..."

"So why don't you? What's stopping you from exploring the world and being all that you want to be?"

"Because I'm scared. It's new and unfamiliar and I've never been there before and," her voice broke and she clenched her hands into tight, little fists, the apple rolled away on the floor. "And I'm doing this alone. I've never been more alone in my life and I have to do this all on my own."

Ray felt an overwhelming desire to scream. How could she explain that the only person standing in the way of her realizing her dreams was, in fact, herself. She was her own worst enemy and really, what do you do with that? She exhaled, "How do you escape yourself?"

She could feel tears prickling her eyes but she held them back, "How do you let go of everything? It's always with me like a dark shadow. Everything. I feel it all. Always, and I don't know how to not feel anymore."

"Write it out," James said without hesitation. "Write it all out. And five, or six years from now if you find it, then you'll look back and admire your ability to turn something this negative into something positive. Even if it's just words running about on a page, at least your thoughts aren't suffocating you. They have a release. Words heal. Words help. They're therapeutic."

Jane had said something like that too, Ray recalled. So did Mary. She looked out the window, the sunlight shone parallelograms of light onto the floor illuminating slow moving speckles of dust in its wake. Temporarily hypnotized, her eyes traced the strange patterns. She knew she should answer James and agree whole heartedly with his suggestion to write it all out, but, what if …

"Franchesca?" Gently he turned her face to his. "What's wrong?"

"What if I have nothing to say?" Ray exhaled in a rushed whoosh of air. "What if I'm just sitting there, pen in hand and nothing comes?" That would be a fate worse than losing her fingers entirely, she'd have lost the ability to articulate how she was feeling.

"Look, you don't have to go to Paris to write about France," he began impatiently.

"So am I doomed to look at guide books with flashy covers and everyone else's holiday pictures?" she snapped.

He exhaled and pinched the bridge of his nose with his long fingers, "No. That's not what I meant."

"Then?"

"All you need is your imagination," he held up his hand as Ray opened her mouth to protest, "It may be cheesy, but I think it's true. You don't need to be a wizard to write about magic or an alchemist to write about the elixir of life, all you need," he gently tapped the side of Ray's head with his finger, "Is that." "James, I'm twenty three years old. Mary's eighteen. Even as we speak she's composing the greatest novel of her time and then there's Jane whose been writing since birth, I can't possibly have anything to say. I seriously doubt if I'm gifted, I'm probably as mental as Van Gogh but if I've never felt the crazy passionate kind of love that would make me want to rip my ear off my head...James, I suck," her shoulders slumped dejectedly. "I can't write. I'm better off being nothing. Drowning in a lake full of nothing. Like Virginia Woolf."

James looked at her, "I had a feeling we would come to Ms. Woolf," he said, a slow smile spreading across his face.

"What do you mean?"

"You live in a time of education and equality and women's rights and the only thing holding you back is your own fear. What would Virginia Woolf say?"

"What?" Ray's head shot up, "Are we going to see her?"

"Why? Are you afraid of Ms. Woolf?" he teased.

"James, you can't be serious," Ray stammered as the carriage came to a halt, "We're actually going to see Virginia Woolf. Now?" her eyes widened with dread, "Please tell me it's not depressed Virginia Woolf, and slightly happy Virginia Woolf, circa 1930."

"She's alive, in a pretty good mood and I believe just

about to take a walk by the University," James said, stepping out the carriage into the sunlight. He gallantly bowed and extended his hand to Ray, "Coming?"

Chapter VII
A Fish out of Water

As Ray stepped out of the carriage once more, in the blink of an eye, they had traveled through time. Smoggy air and the acrid smell of the Thames greeted her as she stood on tiptoes to observe their new surroundings. On one side was the hustle of London street cars and on the crowded pavements little boys and girls ran through the traffic, their faces smudged with soot. It was something out of a Dickens novel. A cool wind lifted the hair off her neck and made her shiver. She turned to her right and saw the sprawling green lawn of what looked like a university.

The thrill of slipping into another walk of life was overwhelming. She could scarcely believe she was in an age where her great grandparents were growing up. It was everything her mother had shown her in fragile, carefully preserved photographs. It was everything and more because here she was experiencing it for herself.

Would her mother ever believe this? She inhaled the London air deeply and hugged her sides. It was completely magical being a time traveler. The sensation of being somewhere completely new was exhilarating and, Ray noted with a delighted smile, the sensation of *wearing* something new was definitely fun. "Not bad at all," she murmured looking down at her high-waisted pants and printed peach blouse; a thick strand of pearls looped around twice over her neck clattered noisily. Ray lifted the back of her right foot to examine the heel on her shoe, "Quite high for the 20's," she observed, with a little backwards kick.

She turned at the sound of James re-emerging from the carriage, where he had left instructions with the driver. "And what do you look like?"

Knowing James, he would probably look like the ideal poster boy of the 1920's. Looking as immaculate in whatever time they were in, James always blended in perfectly. Especially now in his neat Oxford pants, light blue vest and a casual brown jacket slung over his shoulders, he raised his fedora hat grandly, "We are at the pinnacle of sophistication and high fashion."

"I thought that was a daily thing for you," she teased, unpinning her nametag from her blouse. It was becoming second nature, she thought with a little smile as she handed it to James for safekeeping. "Tag."

"Tag." He affirmed.

"Book?"

"Right here," he said tapping the front of his shirt.

Her head suddenly felt heavy and Ray reached up and pulled a hat off her own head, "How am I supposed to wear this?" The large helmet-like hat in her hands sat there adorned with a large purple ribbon at the side. A hat like this wouldn't last more than ten minutes with her.

"You keep your chin high and look down your nose at anyone and anything, naturally," he grinned, adjusting her hat properly. "It's the look that defined an era." His fingers trailed along the side of her neck as he tucked her hair neatly away into her hat, her vision temporarily obscured by its wide brim.

His touch always made her shiver with an enchanted happiness and she swatted his hand away, really it wouldn't do to have these kinds of physical reactions. Especially not in the 1920's when they were in the thick of women's suffrage.

"Cold?" he asked, misinterpreting the reaction his touch had on her. "It's the changing of the seasons." Small yellowing trees lined the well-manicured university lawn and scattered all over the grass were browning, red leaves. Ray saw two large buildings on either side of the campus and a clearing where she could hear the distinct flowing water of a nearby lake.

"Slightly." It was a chilly day, even the sun had disappeared behind the clouds.

"A bit of brisk walking should get the blood running in your veins." James tucked her gloved hand in his own and led her towards the clearing by the pond. His normal walking pace had slowed down to match hers, Ray noticed with a surge of affection, thinking back to how she would trail after him when they had first met. *Or maybe he realizes how clumsy I am and wearing two inch heels isn't exactly helping,* she thought with a grin as she looped her arm in his.

The far side of the campus was flooded with people in general or to be more accurate, Ray thought her eyes narrowing, flooded with *men*. She lifted her chin high and walked beside James, reminding herself that she too belonged here despite the obvious lack of female population. "Times have changed so much," she said softly, thinking fondly of her own university and the diversity of their student population.

"They had to," James replied.

"Well, well, what do we have here?" A man in a gray suit and oily voice came towards them. He wore a bowtie which he kept fingering in a twisted way and a moustache too large for his face. He leered at Ray with shrewd pale eyes, putting his face close to hers, "Come to play with the big boys, little girl?"

She felt movement at her side and saw the stranger's pale eyes widen with fright as James lunged towards him, "Oh bloody hell!" he bellowed and ran off, tripping over his shoes.

Ray pulled James back before he tore the man into pieces, "James, he's not worth it. Pity he's not getting the education he's in dire need of attaining," she remarked, adjusting the collar of James' shirt.

James put a possessive arm around Ray, "He's lucky you stopped me," he said darkly, watching the retreating figure hurry across the lawn.

"Maybe you altered his future self to make him an advocate for women's rights. Did you see how fast he ran?" Ray laughed.

"You really do find everything funny, don't you?" James said wryly, looking at her smiling face.

"I mean, James, I *was* locked in a bathroom in a house full of the most elite dead poet's society to date," Ray felt goose bumps prickle her skin as she recalled the pale vision she had seen in the mirror.

"You were very brave," James said, squeezing her hand.

"So were you just now." Ray bit back a smile, she was secretly pleased that he wanted to defend her honor, it was so old fashioned and romantic. She cleared her throat before he caught her smiling to herself and nuzzled her cheek into his shoulder, "It's the thought that counts, James," she said admiration shining in her voice. He really was her hero.

They continued strolling through the lawn where the crowd gradually thinned out as they entered a clearing when suddenly a tall figure clad in a grey dress walked straight past them, her cloche hat bouncing with each incensed step she took. Her bun had come undone and grey hair fanned around her back like angry wings ready for flight. Ray's heart lurched as she stared after the retreating woman who could only be Virginia Woolf.

She felt a tug and realized she was being pulled towards the direction Virginia Woolf had gone in. "James, what are you doing?" Ray hissed, grabbing his arm. She still hadn't gotten used to the sensation of his skin, it was like electricity under her fingertips. "Do you mind?"

He paused and stopped walking, "You're right. Absolutely right. We should go back. Why would you want to talk to Virginia Woolf?"

Virginia Woolf.

Ray felt like she was having an outer body experience, which, in retrospect, she probably was, but in this moment, in this time here she was and there was Virginia Woolf. "James!" her nails dug into his arm, "You can't just barge in and disturb the woman, she's already more than a little disturbed."

"Awful joke, Franchesca," he grinned, his hand on hers as he pried her fingers gently off his sleeve.

"I wasn't being funny," she whispered back, her tone prickly. As they approached her, Ray knew that there was no mistaking who the woman was, she had seen that pensive profile so many times on book covers. But she had always looked either contemplative or melancholy, a hint of sadness etched around her eyes. Today, Ray thought anxiously nibbling on her fingernail, she looked angry.

"Maybe we shouldn't intrude," Ray said in a panicky voice, "James, she's by a lake, what if she decides to go for a stroll in it!" She turned to him, her eyes wide with shock, "James, can we save her from drowning herself?" Deep down she knew that Virginia wouldn't take her own life until many years later, until her depression would come back once more, until the voices would start again. "James, can we tell her not

155

to?" she asked in a small voice.

He shook his head remorsefully, "We can't do any such thing." Leading Ray to the other side of the lake where Virginia had sat down crossly, he pulled Ray down on the grass in front of him, his legs on either side of her. She leaned into his arms and watched as Virginia sat crossly opposite them.

"But..."

"No buts. I've given up asking you to not talk to your literary idols, but you absolutely cannot say anything that will alter them. That will have an irrevocable effect on the time continuum." He exhaled, "I do expect you to follow the basic rules of time travel, but I don't expect you to understand."

"Does that have anything to do with a flux capacitor?"

"What?"

Ray flipped her hair over her left shoulder, "I don't expect you to understand."

"Why don't you stop flirting with me and go talk to her?" he asked, his breath tickling her ear.

"James, really, I don't think she'd approve of having two twenty something's gawking at her."

"I've never seen you gawk." He cupped her face in his

156

hands and tilted her head back, "What does it look like?"

"I gawk at you all the time."

James grinned, "I know."

"James, honestly you are so..." A sudden movement caught her eye and her voice trailed off as her eyes transfixed themselves on the lone figure across the pond. The whisper of the willows nearby was lulling her into a trance, it felt like a dream of which she was a mere spectator. She felt hypnotized. "James, I can't talk to her," she whispered.

James leaned forward, "Why not? I believe she was a passionate advocate for women to speak their minds and talk. Even if it was in her presence," he teased.

Ray looked at the lake and noticed glimmers of gold streaking through the water. A little fish jumped up and darted about once again. "James! Is this the part where she's sitting by the bank in 'A Room of One's Own'?" her voice filled with wonder as she recollected the first chapter of her favorite essay by Woolf.

Ray recalled how riveted she had been when her professor at Bath had revealed the genius behind Virginia Woolf's great essay. When asked to lecture the women at the Arts Society at Newham and the Odtaa at Girton about

157

women and fiction, Virginia had drawn inspiration from her own life and the blatant barriers she had come across imposed by men. One such incident occurred at the University where she had dreamt up at imaginary character called Mary Beton who would seek to discover women's role as artists as well as their responsibility to themselves to subvert their male counterparts and excel in the world of fiction. Women, Woolf had argued, were just as capable as men and deserved the same rights and privileges that their male counterparts were born into.

"So wait," Ray's eyebrows furrowed as she tried to remember when Virginia Woolf had published her lecture, "Are we in 1930?"

"Close." He leaned his chin on her shoulder as they both looked out at the silhouette of the agitated writer, "1929."

"It just vexes me!" came Virginia's crisp voice from across the pond. She had flopped down by the banks, her hair spread across the grass, her hands balled up into fists.

"What's vexing?" Ray called out before she could stop herself, she leaned forwards as far as her body would let her; James held her back from completely tumbling into the water.

"The minds of people, vex me," Virginia said sitting up to

158

look at Ray, "Every day they seem to grow smaller and paler with such indifference to others that they lose their color of imagination entirely!"

Ray yearned to tell her it wouldn't be like this forever, that schools would thrive with a mixed female population, that women would be equally blessed with the rights that they should have known since birth. But all she could do was listen.

"Has something happened?" James asked, his green eyes clouded with concern.

She exhaled and sat up straight, her neck high as though commanding their natural surroundings to sit and take notice of what she was about to say. "Only the Fellows and Scholars are allowed here; the gravel is the place for me," she said, her eyes flashing fire. "My thoughts, flutter like this fish, in and out, hither and thither, and how insignificant they seem upon the banks of this land but yet, how full of promise and imagination, and this *man*," she spat out, "This *Beadle* rose to intercept me as I was on my way to the library."

"Why?" Ray said, breathlessly, hanging onto every word she spoke.

"Because I do not belong here, I am a woman. I am best

kept in the kitchen or sewing or twiddling my thumbs, or perhaps seated at a luncheon with my remarks restricted primarily to the weather," she expelled a great breath, "And yet, women have written thousands of books, thousands of thoughts imprinted, immortalized forever and kept out of reach!" Her voice shook with barely suppressed rage. "What troubled times are these when a woman is unable to live as free as a man, based on biological grounds alone."

Ray's heart went out to the frustrated woman in grey on the grass. How she longed to reassure her that one day all these trials and tribulations would vanish and the times would change dramatically from what a woman was expected to be to what a woman herself could choose to be. "It will change," she said, her voice strong with conviction, "They can't keep us on the grass forever."

Virginia turned to Ray with a ghost of a smile, "And yet on the grass we are," she said her voice laced with irony. She looked at Ray curiously as though truly noticing her for the first time, "How did you get to be here?"

"I choose to sit by the grass," Ray said carefully, "And if I choose to I shall find a way to be surrounded by thousands of books in the library that the Beadle refused you."

"A radical," Virginia said her face lighting up pleasantly, "What do you stand for?"

"Equality," Ray answered. "And intelligence. Too often we are overshadowed by ignorance based on another's opinions with no deliberation or research of our own to verify the truth. Too often we have what some might call the truth, gift wrapped and handed to us, and we are unable to determine if it is real or a fabrication."

Virginia nodded passionately, "We are kept from exploring. From earning!" her voice darkened, "We live on what either our husbands give us, or what our fathers give us because we are too impoverished to entertain the notion of independence," she scowled at the grass, "What had our mothers been doing then that they had no wealth to leave us? Powdering their noses? Looking in at shop windows? Flaunting in sunlight at Monte Carlo? Here between the shade of a dwindling October afternoon, here where anything is possible, we are resigned to our fates, when all we need is a room of our own and five hundred pounds to maintain independence of residence and thought. No force in the world can take me from my five hundred pounds. Food, house and clothing are mine forever," she finished, her head held

161

majestically.

Ray was sure her mouth had dropped open in awe and her eyes felt glazed as she heard her idol's infamous words spoken form her own lips. James was equally entranced by the woman before them.

Virginia Woolf turned to James with an imperiously raised eyebrow, "Do you find my thoughts too radical for your tastes, young man?"

James smiled, "Not at all, I thoroughly enjoy them, actually, Ms. Woolf."

"How refreshing," she beamed. Her whole face lit up and the world was right again.

Her moods, Ray noted, were as changing as the waves; one moment calm and controlled and the next wild and untamed, but there was an underlying rhythm to them, she thought, watching her bask in the bright sunshine, all she wanted was the freedom to do as she liked, to think as she liked, a right that people took for granted in her time.

"Do you write?" she asked Ray.

"Well, I..." Ray began. She attempted to write, did that count? How feeble that would sound.

"Actually, it's a work in progress," James said pulling out

Ray's blue book from his jacket pocket.

It was incredible to her that he could be so smooth and charming when she was flustered and floundering for words. With a grateful look, she took the book from him and held it up so Virginia could see it across the little stretch of bank that separated them.

"And what do you like to write?" she asked smiling down curiously at the velvet book.

"Fiction." Ray answered promptly. "The world of dreams is far more real to me than the reality in which we live. Sometimes." She thought of Jane Austen's hope for love poured into her novels and Mary's own nightmares realized in Frankenstein. "There is nothing that is thought that can't be written."

"If we live to see another century or so," Virginia said, stretching out on the bank, her brooding eyes closed. "And have five hundred a year, each of us and rooms of our own; if we have the habit of freedom and the courage to write exactly what we think; if we escape a little from the common-sitting room and see human beings not always in their relation to each other but in relation to reality, the sky, and the trees or whatever it may be, in themselves," she exhaled and turned to

Ray and James with hope in her tired eyes, "There would be no limit for what we could do."

Ray hugged her knees close to her chest, digesting every word. "There is no limit to what we can do. We're not just fish out of water, we belong here, on this grass and in those buildings," she turned to look at the silhouette of the library against the dark sky, "Wherever we choose. There is no limit. The Beadle cannot tell us so."

Virginia stood up abruptly, brushing the grass off her skirt, "You are correct." Her long fingers twisted her hair into a neat elegant bun and placed her hat upon it smartly, "This is the world of reality, not men and women, and anything *is* possible." She turned to Ray with a smile that lit up her whole face, "How nice to meet a youth who believes as passionately as I. And you," she gave James an appraising look, "You are a rarity. Well, goodbye."

"Goodbye, Ms. Woolf," Ray said sitting up. How she longed for more time with her, more minutes, hours, anything. But what she had was enough. What she had no one could take away, she sighed as she watched one of the most influential women in the history of literature walk away .The desire to race after her was overwhelming. When suddenly she turned back and looked at Ray, "Keep writing. There is much joy and freedom in the written word," and with a brisk click of her heels Virginia Woolf disappeared into the trees as suddenly as she appeared coming out of them.

Ray sighed and leaned back against James, entwining her fingers in his. "Did that really happen?" she asked softly.

"Everything really happened." She could hear the smile in his voice.

She looked at her blue book once more; the cover was clear and unchanging. *Could she write?* Not as brilliantly as Austen or Shelley or Woolf, but they were of a different era, perhaps it was time to stop comparing herself to the ones she admired and perhaps in order to become like them in her own way, she would have to rise from the ashes of dusty words and fragmented poems and become a literary phoenix in her own right.

"Pen?" James asked, offering one from his pocket.

"Is there anything you don't have?" Ray smiled, accepting the silver pen. It was heavy and elegant. Ray only hoped the words she drew from the ink were half as nice as the instrument itself. She absently chewed on the end of it as she contemplated the blank page before her.

What could she say? What could she write?

James lay back on the grass, his knees on either side of Ray, "Wordsworth once said, to fill your paper with the breathings of your heart."

Her pen lifted of its own accord and began scratching the paper,

There's a need to break free,

Untangle this mess

Through words and song

My soul starts to undress.

She sighed and stared at the page. *Why was she being so melancholic? Was it possible to write a happy poem that wasn't thick with nostalgia?* She felt like a bad rendition of Wordsworth, minus the French mistress and illegitimate child.

What was wrong with her? Usually she couldn't wait to start writing but now it was as though she had nothing to say.

No. That wasn't right. There was much to say. Much too much. But the words wouldn't come. They slipped away somewhere between her thoughts, uncultured by her pen. She groaned.

Here she was, in a perfect place in time, surrounded by light, beauty and a halo of something as she could only describe as magic, and yet, Ray continued chewing the end of her pen, and yet she wasn't inspired to write about the future. She was stuck in the past, a past that cut her deep. Gone were the days of childhood, the laughter had ceased. The flowers would continue their cycles, they would change with the seasons, with Time, with the world, but she couldn't change. She couldn't adapt to change and Time was a bad joke, mocking her through it all.

"What happened?" James asked, the warmth of his arms around her once more. "You've been quiet for so long, I thought you were penning the next great novel."

"That's a laugh," Ray said, closing her book firmly. She flopped on her back and squinted up at the clouds for a sign, an image, some kind of reassurance that everything would be alright. She felt James lie beside her, his fingers entwined in her own.

She closed her eyes. If she could just have this. This perfect moment. These perfect memories then maybe she could find her voice and put pen to paper and actually express her thoughts and hopes and dreams and aspirations.

James' voice broke her out of her silent contemplation, "What was university like for you?"

Ray slowly opened her eyes, "It was good."

"Oh, lovely, you've really painted a picture for me."

Ray laughed. "It was good. Really good, actually," she shook her head, "You'd think that after four years in a somewhat prestigious English program, I could think of a better adjective," she yawned and rubbed her eyes. "It was brilliant, really great. I just," she shrugged helplessly, "I went in to be a writer and I came out still wanting."

"You have so much faith in everyone else," he said shaking his head, "In people you've never even met, but when it comes to you, you're so unsure." He sounded so disappointed in her, so aggravated, she could feel her eyes begin to prickle with frustration.

"You don't understand, James. I just don't know if I can find this ability to create something out of words."

"That which you seek is already within you," he whispered holding her hand.

Ray turned away from James and surveyed the clouds with a renewed sense of determination, surely there had to be something good out there that wasn't laden with disappointment or misery. Her dark eyes scanned the sky for a shape, a sign, but all she saw were broken clouds, their white foam stretching across the iridescent sky.

Chapter VIII
Yellow Brick Road

They decided to go for a walk before it got too dark. The carriage had ambled away and it was just them and the pale night. Past the foggy streets of London, around the bend where the paved road gave away to a grassy trail, to a familiar place Ray knew she had been before.

She absently crunched on the salted chestnuts James had bought her from a street vendor earlier. The tangy salt was making her thirsty and she made a mental note to find a flask the next time they slipped in another era to meet someone. Ray wiped her hands absently on her jeans...*wait jeans*? She was just wearing those high-waisted pants earlier. Her eyes flew over her surroundings. When she inhaled the sweet musk of flowers, she knew James had taken her back to where they had first met. Even in the growing darkness she recognized the trees and the silvery lake where they had been, what seemed now, a lifetime ago. And yet somehow as she looked down at her clothes with a soft cry, it was all the same. The clothes she had been wearing the morning before in her shop, had magically reappeared once more, from her worn orange shoes to her name tag tattered as ever, was placed exactly where it should be.

Why were they back here? Why was he so quiet? Were they going back? Her heart froze. *Was it over?* For the first time she knew what she wanted, she was just afraid that it wouldn't come true if she said it aloud. *But that was crazy, wasn't it?* Superstitious, even. Supernatural fears based on an unorthodox reality. Not real.

But still...

"You've got that look again," James said, smiling at her as they continued walking.

She turned, self-consciously tucking a piece of stray hair behind her ear, "What look?"

"The look where you want to say something but think several times before you should, but eventually say it anyway. Just cut out the middle man. Tell me."

When did he know her so well that he knew what her looks meant? Well after his little observational speech the last time they were here about her lack of love for technology, Ray knew she shouldn't be surprised when he knew what every nuance of her expression meant.

She regarded him as discreetly as she could for a few

moments longer, the moonlight and shadows working in her favor. He really is quite perfect for you, the thought floated in her mind and then vanished. No, he was James. Her companion. And Ray always thought she was incapable of having any sort of emotional connection to anything that wasn't a dusty book as of late.

And yet...

"Just say it," he said, his voice tinged with amusement.

"You're going to think I'm this self-involved, overly sensitive, absolutely lost soul," Ray confessed weakly.

"Nope," he responded, shaking his head almost comically.

Yeah, right. "Yup," she mirrored his actions, nodding her head.

"Well, you'll never really know unless you tell me, right?" His smile was infectious. "Go on, it can't be that bad." He led them to a grassy slope, took his jacket off and laid it on the ground. He patted the spot next to him as he sat down, stretching his long legs in front of him. Ray walked over tentatively and sat down beside him. He gave her an encouraging smile, "Go on."

Ray crossed her arms over her chest, "Why can't we talk about you for a change, all we ever do is talk about me."

"Because I'm here to listen and I truly have nothing half as fascinating to say."

"Liar."

"Nope."

"Tell me your secrets."

"Ask me your questions."

"Really?"

"Maybe. You go first."

"Fine." Ray was torn between speaking her mind, telling him the depths of her innermost thoughts and let her words speak themselves, or just playing her feelings of anxiety off as being hungry. He might even believe her if she said she was starving. She sighed, well she never could keep quiet for very long, so why start now?

"I don't know sometimes, I don't think I'm strong enough to move on with my life," Ray said in a rush, keeping her eyes focused on the rusted swing before her.

"You managed to be in the same room as Jane Austen and you didn't kidnap her, that has to show some strength of character," he said wryly. "And discipline."

Ray chuckled, "I know, I still can't believe that happened," she turned to him, eyes shining, "The whole day has been

173

pretty unbelievable." Their faces inched closer and all she could think was how *he* was pretty unbelievable. It wasn't just his obvious physical beauty, there was something about him that made her feel so safe and protected. His eyes were burning into hers once more and she realized with a sudden stammer of her heart that she had memorized every angle of his face, every shade of his green eyes. Her breath caught and she bit her lip.

James was the first to turn away, running a hand through his thick hair in agitation.

Ray quickly averted her gaze as well and cleared her throat. "Sorry," she murmured.

"For what?"

For wanting to look at you forever. "I don't know."

James gave her an affectionate smile, "Then don't apologize."

"Sorry," she grinned mischievously.

"Oh, Franchesca, what do I do with you?"

"Don't make me climb up the Swiss countryside for starters," she joked, nudging him with her shoulder. They laughed, their shoulders touching and once more a silence fell over them as she found herself searching his face for answers

174

for questions she was too afraid to ask.

James leaned back on his elbow, putting a fraction of distance between them. "But coming back to the real issue at hand," he began smoothly, "What's so bad about the real world?"

Well, for starters, you're not in it, she wanted to say. Averting her eyes quickly from his she stared out at the lake in front of her. The shimmering water was a pale silver, ripples of moonlight spilling across the surface. A cool breeze perfumed with the scent of wild flowers fluttered through her hair and once again she thought they had found a little piece of Paradise somewhere in Time. She turned to him, "James, do you believe in soul mates?" she asked, trying to keep her voice neutral.

He paused. "Ideally, yes. But real life seldom obliges us with Romanticised notions such as soul mates, unfortunately."

"But...no, I don't believe that," Ray shook her head. *That was impossible.* "I refuse to believe that."

"Why?"

"Because I've believed in it my whole life," she said simply.

"Well, where did you first get the idea of a soul mate?"

Beauty and the Beast? Romeo and Juliet? Both answers seemed quite lame spoken aloud. How could she explain that if a woman and a grotesque monster could fall in love that there was hope for her, that if the love Romeo and Juliet felt for one another could transcend death, that there too was hope for her. But those were just books, plays, fairy tales. Not real life.

All she had known of love was in the pages of a book, how it brought her to the heights of rapture then made her crumble back to the earth with the reality of her existence, her mouth filled with dust, her head brimming with memories, burdened with thoughts, burdened with pangs of longing that tore into her beating heart.

What did her heart beat for anymore? It just beat. An unconscious command sent by her brain making it pump blood throughout her body.

That was science.

Where did feeling fall into play?

What did her heart beat for? Beyond the biology of her being, skin and bones, flesh and blood, what was her purpose?

She turned to him, her eyes the colour of fallen stardust, full of tears, "James, what am I living for?"

"Don't get tragic on me, young lady," he said sternly, gently tucking a tendril of stray hair behind her right ear, "Franchesca, you have so much to live for, you've got ..."

"A mother who thinks I'm mental, friends who think I've forgotten them and books!" she finished with a soft cry, burying her head on her knees, "All I've got James are books and they're not real." She could feel his hand stroking her back in comforting circles, and choked back the sob that was threatening to escape her lips.

"Please don't cry."

"I don't like leaking like this," Ray hiccupped. She wiped her cheeks with the back of her hand and looked up at him, "James am I doomed to be Virginia Woolf? Or someone like Jane Austen? Minus the talent, though. Someone who never experiences the throes of love beyond a description, beyond a page? Is that why you brought me here?"

He didn't respond.

"Is that why you're taking me back? Because that's why we're here, right?"

Silence.

"Please say something." It was as though he had completely shut down. Like a robot. If there was only some way to make him understand... a glimmer of an idea began to take shape into her mind. "Wait! James, if I have to leave, maybe...maybe you can come too?" Her voice grew more excited with the thought. Of course there would have to be some sort of explanation she would eventually give her mother, she couldn't just parade around with a boy living in her bookshop. She turned to him her eyes alight with excitement. "You could live with me," she paused, "I mean, if you want to," she added, shyly realizing that perhaps she was assuming too much on his behalf and that she was being quite bold on her own.

"Franchesca," his voice came out taught and stoic. "I can't." He stood up and stepped away from her.

"Okay, so we'll find you someplace else to live. Finding a place in Bath isn't the easiest, but I'll help you. I mean, you can't be locked up here forever, can you?" she turned in a circle, her arms outstretched, "This can't be it for you. Surely you must have come from somewhere." Her cheeks were starting to hurt from smiling so much, "Right?"

He remained silent.

Her smile faltered, "Right?"

James shook his head slowly, "Franchesca, I don't belong

in your world. I belong here."

"What do you mean?"

"I belong here in this time."

"Where the hell *is* here, James?" Ray exploded. "Tell me! Where are we? This isn't real, it has to be some sort of dream, and yet," she reached up and touched his face with her fingers, "And yet, you're here, and you're real. Human." She placed her palms on his chest, his heart was an erratic beat beneath her hands. "This is the most alive I've ever felt. And I'm not even reading Pride and Prejudice."

He chuckled softly into her hair and pressed his forehead against hers, "You're funny."

"It's the truth, James. I've never felt this alive before."

"You are alive," he enunciated each word carefully, his eyes burning into hers.

Of course she was. She had to be. She had never felt more human than this moment. She closed her eyes feeling his hand cup her cheek. His touch set her alight in a way no poem ever had. It wasn't words, it was real.

"Franchesca, you're alive," he repeated gently.

Ray looked up at him with liquid eyes, "And you?" she whispered.

His mouth tightened into a grim line and he shook his head, "Not in the same way you are."

Something inside her snapped. *What was he talking about?* How could he stand there calmly when his words were causing her world to shatter in a million pieces. "What do you even mean? Then where are we? How did we get here? And how can you breathe and talk and walk and touch me and not be alive? Who are you? What figment of my treacherous imagination dreamt you up?" She was almost afraid to look at him, "Where did you come from? You say you can travel through time and you take me to places I've only dreamed about. You showed me things that I would never be able to see on my own. I met Jane Austen! You do realize this, don't you? Jane bloody Austen!" Her head was pounding as she desperately tried to grasp the unravelling fabric of his words for some semblance of truth and logic. "Did I read you somewhere? Did I see you somewhere? Have I met you before?" her eyes filled with frustrated tears, "I would've known, James. I would've remembered."

He regarded her with a pained expression but spoke not a word.

"What are you?" Ray spun around to face him, her hair

flying like a wild, angry mane, "What manner of creature are you?" For the first time she felt afraid of him but a curious rage had overtaken her sensibilities. "Was it all just a lesson then?" Averting her gaze from him Ray hugged her chest tightly willing herself not to cry. She could feel her heart exploding inside her. "Did you bring me here to show me what a failure I am compared to all these great women? You needn't have bothered, I know I can't write. I'll never be able to write like them, I'll be trapped forever in someone else's words and someone else's story..." her voice broke and hot tears slipped down her cheeks.

"That's not true." In a flash he was there, his lips hot against her hair, his arms around her, his touch reassuring, "You know that's not true."

Ray kept her eyes squeezed shut, maybe it would be easier to say this without looking at him. It was as though he had parted the Red Sea and all the emotional baggage she had kept reserved for a blowout therapy session was flooding out, for better or for worse. And yet, she inhaled the scent of him deeply, she had never felt calmer as the storm continued to rage within her.

"It's ok," he whispered soothingly.

"No it's not," Ray hiccupped. *How could it be?* "It hasn't been okay in so long."

"Darkness doesn't last forever."

"Then come back with me."

He ran an agitated hand through his hair, "You need to find the yellow brick road that takes you back where you belong, it's different for each of us."

"James, you can't leave."

"Franchesca, you know I can't stay."

"Why?" Her eyes desperately searched his, "I don't belong anywhere else, you do realize that don't you? You're telling me to find a yellow brick road to go back to somewhere where I don't belong. I don't fit in anywhere, I'm like an emo kid without the exaggerated eyeliner and the bad music." She paused and smiled sadly, "You wouldn't understand." *How could he?* He was so sure of himself, of who he was, of what he wanted. "How could someone like you understand someone like me?" she whispered to herself, hiding her face.

"You're not an emo kid," he said, gently tucking a piece of stray hair behind her ear. She could hear a glimmer of a smile in his voice. "You're so much more than that."

"Tell me then, what was the point of it all. Was I meant to

182

have some grand epiphany? Something that would change my life," she could feel her heart wrenching against her chest, "Why did you bring me here?"

"Some lessons can't be learnt in books alone. You have to feel them," James said patiently, closing his eyes in frustration.

"Don't tell Aesop that, he'll have wasted his time then," she mumbled.

"As to how you came here, well Franchesca, you brought yourself here," he began carefully, his voice solemn. "You're not dreaming. This place does exist, as does Darcy and Frankenstein, but also, Franchesca, equally as important, are the women who created them; Jane and Mary and Virginia. You've been unable to reconcile yourself with anyone or anything remotely separate from the printed word and you seem to have forgotten that these remarkable women who dreamed up these remarkable characters were also remarkable people in their own right," his gaze penetrated her own with a wisdom far beyond his years. "Franchesca, you've forgotten how to be a person."

It was as though a knife was cutting into her heart with each word James had spoken. The logical part of her mind was screaming for reason, for justice, for the indignant response that had flown to her lips when he had begun talking, and now it was the same part of her mind that had shamed her into the reality of her situation. She had readily resigned herself to a life void of any meaning beyond the care of her father's book store, she didn't feel the need to reconnect with her mother or her friends because she was comfortably trapped in the stories of others that...Franchesca clasped a hand to her mouth, she had forgotten to live her own tale.

"James, I -"

"Franchesca, I know how beautiful books are and I know how the very words on a page can ignite the deepest recesses of your imagination alight with possibility and hope. And I know, too, how safe books are to you. That they are truly your sanctuary, your friends, but -" he traced the curve of her cheek with his finger, "There's loneliness in that refuge."

"James, look," she pushed her hair back with both hands in an attempt to regain some sense of lost control. "I don't do the whole damsel in distress thing."

"How terribly modern of you." He attempted to bite back a smile.

She resisted the urge to stamp her foot like a three year old throwing a tantrum. Willing whatever lessons she had learned from her brief stint in hot yoga to repress her desire to scream and refocused her energy on positive feelings and thoughts. "The point is, James, I didn't think I needed saving, or rescuing, or a knight errant, or anything of the sort, until you," she could feel her throat constrict and her voice crack but she knew she had to keep going, "And you helped me, James, in ways that I could never imagine, so what I'm trying to say is that I need you. You can't leave me and perhaps I've lost all credibility with the modern woman who doesn't need a man, but I need you. You're more real to me than anything I've ever known," her voice trembled with tears. This was the biggest confession she had ever made to anyone. But she believed in him more than any book she had ever read "James, please don't leave me," she whispered.

He exhaled. "You have so much to live for, so much yet to do."

"But what am I supposed to do when being with you is the only thing that makes me feel alive. Please just try to come back with me. Or leave me here. This space in-between Time feels more like home to me than any place I've ever known. Please, don't say no," she whispered seeing the unrelenting expression on his face, "I've never asked anything of anyone.

And even now James, I just want you to stay with me."

"I can't promise anything now," he hesitated, "In time your view might change, Franchesca." James ran an agitated hand through his unkempt hair. "You have to trust me."

"Why?"

"I'll find you, somehow. I swear, but I can't promise anything. But," he hesitated, "It may not be the same. Time makes fools of us all and perhaps when we do meet again, you won't recognize me at first. You need to have faith," he whispered, his green eyes stormy with emotion, "Try."

Ray averted her eyes and shook her head, "I can't see faith, James. I can't touch it. It's not tangible and maybe it's real for some people, but I need something I can see, something that won't just be a memory I'm holding onto at night when I can't sleep."

"Franchesca, I can't travel back with you, not now. It won't work." He tilted her chin up with his hands, forcing her to meet his gaze, "At least look at me."

"How do you know unless you try?" she said her eyes shimmering with frustrated tears, "Please. Just try. I know I'm not dreaming, I'm never been so awake my whole life and I'm feeling everything as though it's for the first time," she paused,

"Actually, it probably is for the first time. But the point is, James, if this can happen, if we somehow ended up in Hampshire and in Lord Byron's living room and sit by the lake with Virginia Woolf, then I know that anything's possible."

"I can't," he said, his mouth a tight line.

"Yes you can!" Ray cried. "You can change my book into any novel, you can change my clothes in the blink of an eye, you can -"

"I can't. I can't go back with you. I'm not this grand magician!" He pinched the bridge of his nose and closed his eyes. He exhaled slowly, "I'm not a magician, Franchesca," he repeated woodenly.

"You're magic to me," she whispered brokenly looking down at her curled up hands.

They sat in anguished silence watching the moonlight ripple across the lake, its reflection turning silver. Ray couldn't bear to look at him. She didn't know what to say, she had said enough already and it was clear that he couldn't come back with her, she couldn't ask him to anymore. Searing tears slipped down her cheeks onto her lap, like rain. *How could she allow herself to leave? How could he let her go? How could it not mean anything to him when it meant everything to her?* She swallowed thickly. *Was this what it felt like to have your heart truly broken?* Another experience she learnt today but not through the pages of a book, but by the hands of this boy who was staring straight ahead avoiding her. She bit back a sob and felt her body grow rigid with anger. *What right did he have to somehow bring her here, change her entire world and not even offer a sliver of truth as to why he couldn't come back.*

A low growl escaped her throat at the injustice of it all.

"Do you remember how you came here?" James asked, his voice harsh with controlled emotion.

"I fell," she replied curtly. "It hurt."

"You have to fall again, but it will be less painful this time," he said, turning to her. "You have to fall back in Time once more."

She stared straight ahead refusing to meet his gaze, "Fine."

"Don't make this harder than it already is," he pleaded. She could hear the pain searing in his voice.

"James it shouldn't be hard. I apparently slipped through a crack in Time, you showed me everything I needed to see and now I have to go," she replied stoically, avoiding eye contact. "It is as it should be."

"You don't seem to understand -"

"I understand perfectly," she whirled around to face him, "You don't understand James. It's like...it's like," her voice cracked.

"Breathe."

"It's like when you read this fantastic book and go on an incredible journey...you're still alone. And now for the first time in what feels like forever, I've been on this incredible adventure and I'm not alone. And James," her tear filled eyes turned to him imploringly, "James, I have never felt this way before. I never really expected anything different for myself. I always thought I would be alone. But with you, I'm not lonely and I'm so scared to lose this feeling," she swallowed hard, her gaze lowering to their entwined fingers, "Please don't leave me with nothing but memories to remember you by."

"I want you to be happy. I want you to write your story, and travel the world and not feel alone. But I can't make it happen for you. It's something you have to do yourself." His voice broke in the end and he pressed his forehead against hers, "You have to."

Her vision blurred and all she could see was the darkening of the sky and his green eyes looking at her in a way that no one ever had before. *How was it even possible that this was real, that this was happening?* Things like this never happened to her, things like this had never even happened to her favorite heroines. What had begun as a beautiful dream was now ending in a heartbreaking nightmare. She squeezed her eyes shut willing the intoxicating scent of flowers and grass to remain forever, for him to be there when she opened them. "I just want it to be you."

A cool hand stroked her cheek gently.

"You don't seem to understand that I can't help any of this," James said softly. "I can't change anything, this is all beyond my control. My job is to help lost souls find their way. I'm not human in the same way as you. I can't go back to your world without changing. All I can do is tell you that this is real. Everything that happened to you today was real. That man in the bookshop, the book he gave you, this place, the people you met, me, everything, it all happened, you're not dreaming."

She wanted to ask him how he knew about the old man in her shop but when she parted her lips no words came out. There was so much Ray wanted to ask him, to tell him. This day had been the best day of her entire life and she couldn't relive the memories of it alone, it would be like trying to catch a dream and questioning its reality at the same time. Lost in shades of green she felt like she was drowning in the pools of his eyes. "James, I..."

He held her hand, his jaw taut with emotion, "Me too."

She felt the words unspoken from his lips as the rush of the wind flew in her hair. Everything seemed to be moving so fast though they remained where they were. *Was this how she was supposed to fall?*

"Wait," she unpinned the nametag from her shirt and pinned it onto his cardigan with shaking fingers, "For you." It was a small gift to give in exchange for everything he had helped her to see, but she wanted him to have something of hers that meant more than anything else she could ever give, he had already given her so much.

"Franchesca, no," he began. "It belongs to you, I can't ..."

Ray pressed herself against him, kissing him for the first and last time. His mouth was warm and his lips slanted over hers perfectly and she could taste the salt of tears.

Feeling her heart shatter, the world slipped under her once more and she could only feel the sensation of falling.

Chapter IX
The Reluctant Time Traveller

Ray's eyelids slowly fluttered open. The book that had been on her adventures since the very beginning lay fallen from her open hand on the ground next to her. She winced and sat up, her eyes adjusting to the dwindling sunlight reflected on the pavement. Her shadow grew darker and darker with each passing moment.

"James?" she whispered.

The only reply was a gentle flurry of snow that began falling from the sky. Ray felt frozen, dazed and oblivious to the bite of frost that was slowly numbing her hands. How could he be gone? She wiped her wet eyes with the back of her hand. She remembered in agonizingly, perfect detail every flicker of his eyes, his laugh, his slow curving smile, the taste of his kiss and yet...he was gone. And she was here. She leaned against the back of the steps, her back slumped against the hard stone and exhaled a deep, shuddering breath. Her mind felt as though it was full of fluffy cotton balls. She couldn't remember a thing. But the one thing she did know was that James wasn't here.

He was gone.

To anyone walking by Ray looked like a brooding angel, with her dark hair flowing about her like a halo, her eyes black with sorrow, the sun setting behind her back spreading its light around her like wings.

She felt, however, like absolute hell.

She closed her eyes and bit her bottom lip until she felt the skin break and the tangy taste of blood enter her mouth. Every moment with James had been something out of the ordinary, something magical, something she would never get back again, except through memory. She wiped her eyes with the back of her hand and covered her mouth to keep from crying out loud. *Was it really over? Was he really gone?* She choked back a sob. *Had he even existed?*

A door slammed in the distance and the soft thud of footsteps rang out. "What on earth are you doing here? Why are you sprawled out like that? What's going on?" her mother's voice rang as Eleanor ran outside in her robe and slippers.

Ray grinned weakly as she saw her mother's curlers in her hair, "Oh, you know, just thought I'd come by for a visit," she said casually Her muscles ached and she winced as she stood up and wiped her stinging hands on her jeans.

"Why didn't you call? I would've come back and picked you," Eleanor chided, ushering Ray up the pathway to the house. She took off her robe and draped it around her daughter's snow covered shoulders, "Have you eaten anything? You don't look well," she scrutinized Franchesca under the shade of a lamppost. "You really do look quite pale, Franchesca. Did something happen?"

"No, Mother," Ray said with a sad, little smile. She put her arm around her mother's slim waist as they made their way towards the front steps. "Everything is as it should be."

While Eleanor fussed with towels and linens for the guest room she had always set aside for her daughter, Ray wandered through the hallway, past the main entrance and up the stairs.

Everything looked different to Ray's eyes. Or maybe it was she who had changed. Her mother's house wasn't the way she remembered from her last visit in the summer. Along the walls she saw pictures of herself, Ray as a baby in her mother's arms, Ray riding a red bicycle for the first time, Ray fallen from her bicycle with a big smile and an even bigger cast on her leg.

The smell of freshly baked spice cake wafted through the

kitchen, she could hear the opening credits of the Downton Abbey Christmas special from the living room where a cozy fire crackled merrily. Ray wandered inside towards the fire to warm her chapped hands, when a single stocking above the mantelpiece caught her eye. It was a large, red stocking overflowing with candy canes, chocolate and even a small teddy bear was peeking out holding a glittery Swarovski pen.

It had her name on it, Ray realized with a twinge of guilt, as she tenderly stroked the soft, red exterior of the stocking. Her mother had filled the stocking with lovely little presents for her. And Ray hadn't even been planning on coming round for Christmas. She choked back a small sob at the thought of her mother all alone in this house, with a stocking hung for a daughter that never visited. Maybe her mother was as lonely as she was. Maybe it was Ray's fault.

After Ray had taken a quick shower and changed into one of Eleanor's spare nightgowns, she joined her mother at the kitchen table with a renewed sense of determination that she would make every effort to spend more time with her. Shoving thoughts of James aside to the recesses of her mind, Ray sat at the table and unfolded her napkin. She could still feel the salty aftertaste of the roasted chestnuts that James had bought for her and she quickly tore into a piece of bread to drown out any memories her taste buds had retained before she had a meltdown at the table.

"Quite the appetite," Eleanor noted with a grin.

Ray smiled widely her mouth full, cheeks bulging. "Mmhmm."

"It really is so lovely to see you here, Franchesca," Eleanor said, her voice brimming with emotion. Her mother had spared no expense for the meal tonight, the silver candles at the table were lit, the silverware was polished to a shine and once more Ray realized with a pang, how many meals her mother must have eaten at this table. The same way she herself ate most of her meals in the bookshop. Alone. "It's really good to be here, Mum," Ray said tremulously hoping her voice wasn't shaking too much. What an emotional rollercoaster the last few days had already been. She didn't think she could handle any more tears. She filled her mother's glass with apple cider. "I should come more often."

If Eleanor was surprised at Ray's words she hid it well with a beaming smile, "Anytime you want, darling. My home is your home."

"My shop is your shop," Ray smiled in return.

"You know you can keep living in the shop on weekdays and come stay with me over the weekends," Eleanor said, cutting off a thick slice of turkey and placing it on Ray's plate. "There's so much to do in London, we can go on ghost tours, picnics when the weather gets better, there's even an ice skating rink nearby. Lots to do, darling."

"That sounds like a great idea, Mum," Ray said, her mouth full of mashed potatoes. "Only on one condition," she said, holding her fork up in the air.

"Name it."

"You make me turkey every night."

Over the course of a languid hour though the meal had ended neither Ray nor Eleanor moved from the table. They were too busy chatting and catching up on the daily fragments of life they had missed over the years. Ray was surprised to hear that her mother was thinking of retiring from her job and opening a children's school. "But I thought you weren't too fond of children," Ray said carefully hiding a smile.

"I liked you just fine," Eleanor replied with a wink.

"Actually, you did."

"I still like you," Eleanor pointed out.

"Yeah, you're alright too, I suppose," Ray grinned as she

began gathering their plates and rinsing them at the sink.

"What else have I missed? Planning on climbing Kilimanjaro? Opening a bed and breakfast?"

"Oh!"

Ray looked up from the cutlery she was holding, "Is everything alright?"

"Yes, yes. I just remembered. It really is the most curious thing, Franchesca," Eleanor said with a pause. "A parcel came for you, just moments before you arrived."

"Oh really?" Ray said sleepily. Something about the house and her mother's cooking always lulled her into deep sleep. She needed to sleep, it would be the only way she would be able to stop thinking, to stop remembering. "But doesn't the post stop coming on Christmas Eve?" she asked curiously. Her carrot looked up at her forlornly and she half-heartedly stabbed it with her fork.

"Yes," Eleanor nodded, collecting the glasses, "That's what I thought as well, but nevertheless I left it for you under the tree." She chucked to herself, "He really was an extraordinarily curious fellow."

"Curious, how?" Ray asked as she began to load the dishwasher. It was so strange doing something so domestic when what seemed like moments ago she was lying in the grass conversing with Virginia Woolf. With James.

James. She felt a dull ache in her chest, took a deep breath and forced herself to focus on the comforting clang of the cutlery and her mother's pleasant chatter.

"...the most extraordinary green eyes and the oddest shoes, almost like elves," she finished with a laugh. "I suppose he was just caught up in all the holiday spirit."

Ray dropped the forks with a clatter, "Elf shoes?" she asked, her heart racing. The old man from the shop, the one her mother couldn't see when she was there. Her throat constricted, even James had known about him.

"Mother, what did he leave?" she asked, fighting to keep her voice under control.

"Well," Eleanor said, drying her hands on a kitchen towel, "He said that he was returning something. Something he said you had left with him a long time ago." She led Ray towards the Christmas tree. "I left it here for you," she said softly handing Ray the little present, "I hoped you would come."

"And here I am," Ray said, hugging her mother tightly. She looked down at the tiny present in her hand curiously. Packaged in modest brown paper and tied together with a delicate green ribbon, it fit in the palm of her hand perfectly. With bated breath she carefully peeled away the paper and undid the wisps of ribbon.

"What is it?" Eleanor asked from the tree where she was arranging a plate of cookies and presents.

Wordlessly Ray opened her hand, revealing her nametag.

Eleanor came round and plucked it from Ray's frozen hand, "It looks as good as new, Franchesca," she said examining it carefully, "It looks how it did when you first made it all those years ago," she said with a soft laugh. "But, wait," she turned to her daughter frowning, "How did you lose it in less than a day and then have someone mail it to you?"

Ray shook her head, her mouth dry. "I don't know," she managed to say. "Did the man say anything else? When he'd be back, perhaps?" she asked, her mind whirling, desperate for information. She ran to the window and pulled back the curtains for any trace that the old man had left behind. A clue to his whereabouts.

Eleanor walked over to her daughter and handed the nametag back to her. "No, darling. But," she paused, her eyebrows furrowed with concern, "He didn't look well. I invited him in for a cup of tea but he said he would try and

come back another time perhaps," she shook her head sadly,
   "Such a long trip for such an old man."

   Ray felt as though all the breath was being squeezed out
of her body, like a used tube of toothpaste. *James.* It had to
have been James. All along. He was the man in the shop. He
was the visitor. He ... Ray clasped a hand to her mouth. He
told her that he would try and see her but that it would
jeopardize the rules of Time. And he looked ill. But he said he
wasn't alive the same way she was. *Was he ok?* The thoughts
swirled in her mind like a hurricane, but one thing she knew
for certain was that James wasn't ever coming back. She
wouldn't see him again. He was somewhere else entirely in
another dimension in time, lost to her once more.

   "Are you alright, Franchesca?" Eleanor asked worriedly.

   "Just tired, Mum. I think I'll sit here for a bit, before bed,"
she managed to say, her thoughts a chaotic storm.

   Eleanor yawned, "Sure?"

   "Yeah."

   "Alright love, I'll see you tomorrow morning," she kissed
the top of her head, "Merry Christmas."

   "Merry Christmas, Mum," Ray replied watching her
mother's retreating back as she closed the kitchen lights and

headed up the stairs. The living room was bathed in the soft glow of golden lights shimmering from the tree. She pinned the nametag tenderly on her nightgown and settled beneath the glowing lights of the Christmas tree.

It had been him. Him in the book shop, him all throughout and him tonight. She squeezed her eyes shut. How was it possible? She hadn't aged a day in all their time together and he was older, so much older. She strained to recall his last words to her; he had said he would find her though it would take some time.

And Time had made fools of them both. Her body began to rack with silent sobs, the storm inside her began to brew and she was shaken to the core. Piece by piece Ray began to assemble the sequence of events and it all began to make perfect sense. How James had known about her shop and her passion for reading, how he had been able to change the cover of every book he had given her, how he couldn't go back with her but promised that they would meet again but that it would be completely different and she wouldn't be able to recognize him at first. She clutched her sides, and now, his entire life had passed them by while she had so much left to live. Try as she might, she couldn't reconcile James, her James with the kindly old man in the bookshop. She couldn't.

Her mind refused to accept that James had changed while she had remained exactly the same. And somehow he had always known how it would end.

She hugged her knees to her chest and rested her throbbing head between them, willing herself to breathe.

Her mother had mentioned he hadn't looked well, was he sick? Ill? Her breath caught. *Dying?* But he told her that he wasn't alive in the same way she was. Maybe the laws of death didn't apply to him either. Maybe disguised in a human shroud as an old man was the only way he could visit her outside of the world he brought her to.

Oh, James.

She could feel the piercing sensation of his emerald eyes, the soft pressure of his mouth, his searing kiss on her wrist, the way his lips felt under her finger tips when he was asleep in the carriage, the way he tucked her hair into her cap on the snowy plains, the way they had kissed goodbye...it was as though she had lived a thousand lifetimes with him in two days. A quote she had heard before floated in her mind like Virginia Woolf's fish, squirming out of grasp. Something John Keats had written to his fiancée, Fanny Brawn about the time

they had spent together. Ray closed her eyes and whispered
they had spent together. Ray closed her eyes and whispered
softly to herself, "I almost wish we were butterflies and liv'd
but three summer days - three such days with you I could fill
with more delight than fifty common years could ever
contain."

The days she had spent with James were filled with more
delight, adventure and travel than a hundred common years
could ever hope to encompass.

There comes a point in everyone's life where they reach
the crossroads of who they choose to be and how they decide
to move on to get there. Ray had been lost for so many years
and now, for the first time, she was sure of what she wanted
beyond the pages of a book, beyond the wildest depths of her
imagination; to seize happiness and recognize it, to live for
experiences not lessons, to truly be of the world and not a
mere spectator. And to believe in herself and the breathings of
her heart.

James' last wish had been for Ray to write and travel and,
her breath caught, find a way out of the web of loneliness she
had woven around herself.

Maybe something so wonderful and magical couldn't

happen twice, that someone couldn't make the earth move for her and Time to stand still the way he had. But, she thought with a tender smile, she would leave her heart open to the possibility of something great. After all, time spent with James was something she never could have imagined for herself, maybe there was something more out there for her. She owed it to herself to be open to the possibility of it at least.

Ray reached behind the branches where she had left her blue velvet book as her mother had rushed her into the house. As she pulled it out a silver pen fell from between the pages and clattered on the floor. She swallowed and picked up the pen James had given her. Its sleek silver exterior glittered in the soft light and suddenly, without whim, word or warning, her fingers were flying and pages were turning. Flying over familiars letters, moving at a pace and rhythm of their own. She didn't understand it. It was beyond the realm of her control.

Was it minutes? An hour? Or two? Time once more seemed to stand still and Ray lost all sense of it. Her tears subsided.

She could feel her breath coming out slow and even, somehow she felt calmer.

What? She actually wrote something legible. Her eyes traveled down the little paragraph and through her tears, the colors melted like a rainbow dancing across the page. If she could do as Wordsworth had once said and was able to fill her paper with the breathings of her heart, then maybe she would be heard, and maybe, just maybe she could be saved.

The smell of pine filled her senses as the snow continued to fall gently outside, blanketing the city in a frosted wonderland. Ray gently fingered her nametag once more as her pen fell to the floor, the memory of a green eyed boy lulling her into a wistful sleep where dreams came true and Time was on their side.

Made in the USA
Middletown, DE
23 June 2022

67636246R00123